Tonight she was smokin' and ready for anything

There was a do-me flicker in Tessa's eyes that threatened to knock Gabe flat on his ass. He nodded once, acknowledging her, and went to guide her toward the door. They were already late for the party.

But guiding her would involve touching her. And he knew—even crazed and unthinking as he currently was—that was a bad idea. He dropped his hand and waited for her to open the apartment door herself.

A drop of sweat beaded on the back of his neck.

Trouble. And he'd spotted it right off the bat. He knew Tessa. He knew that tilt in her chin, that kick in her walk. When she got like that... Maybe it was time to stop playing games?

Gabe trapped her between the door and the wall, her lean body tight to his. He could feel every inch of her—the fluttering pulse, the tight nipples, the soft hips. She drew in a breath, soft and shaky, and the air burned. His hands itched to explore and discover this new and marvelously arousing Tessa. Instead, he hung on to the last edge of control that he possessed. But for how long...how long?

Blaze™

Dear Reader,

I confess. I have a weakness for bars. It seems as if particular eras in my life are defined by particular bars because I am a creature of habit—not all of them good! In college it was the Dixie Chicken, the most glorious hole-in-the-wall ever created by man. Anyone who's set foot in that rattlesnake-infested place (and you think I'm kidding) will back me up on this. In those colorful years directly after college we spent hours at TGI Fridays, sitting on a high bar stool, talking about dreams and men (sometimes dreamy men).

When I read about two single guys in New York who opened a salad bar that all the single women flocked to, I laughed. A salad bar. I could trump that, I thought. I would create a bar that was comfortable and classy, give it a long and tawdry history, well stocked with top-shelf liquors and top-shelf men. It was surprisingly easy. My editor wanted three brothers, and I knew they had to be Irish (blame that on my great-grandfather, who I suspect was a frequenter of bars, as well). Gabe, Daniel and Sean, my sexy O'Sullivans. Those are my heroes. I hope you fall in love, because I already have.

Cheers,

Kathleen

KATHLEEN O'REILLY
Shaken and Stirred

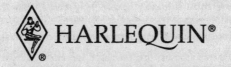

TORONTO • NEW YORK • LONDON
AMSTERDAM • PARIS • SYDNEY • HAMBURG
STOCKHOLM • ATHENS • TOKYO • MILAN • MADRID
PRAGUE • WARSAW • BUDAPEST • AUCKLAND

ISBN-13: 978-0-373-79386-0
ISBN-10:   0-373-79386-3

SHAKEN AND STIRRED

ABOUT THE AUTHOR

Kathleen O'Reilly is an award-winning author of several romance novels who is pursuing her lifelong goal of sleeping late, creating a panty-hose-free work environment and entertaining readers all over the world. She lives in New York with her husband, two children and one rabbit. She loves to hear from her readers at either www.kathleenoreilly.com or by mail at P.O. Box 312, Nyack, NY 10960.

Books by Kathleen O'Reilly

HARLEQUIN BLAZE
297—BEYOND BREATHLESS*
309—BEYOND DARING*
321—BEYOND SEDUCTION*

HARLEQUIN TEMPTATION
967—PILLOW TALK
971—IT SHOULD HAPPEN TO YOU
975—BREAKFAST AT BETHANY'S
979—THE LONGEST NIGHT

*The Red Choo Diaries

With special appreciation
for bartenders everywhere.
I don't know what we'd do without you.

1

WHEN SUMMER BROKE in Manhattan, the sun burned hotter, the days turned muggy, men demanded their beer ice-cold, and women expected the martinis chilled. The sun was setting on one such blistering Thursday evening when the middle-aged female approached the long mahogany bar, a blush on her cheeks and her mouth creased in an apologetic smile.

Gabriel Cormac Silas O'Sullivan, owner, bartender and general patsy of a brother, felt a familiar sense of inescapable doom.

"I think there's a problem with the ladies' room," the woman began. "For the last ten minutes the door's been locked, and there's…moaning coming from inside. Sometimes female, sometimes male. I think there's something lewd going on in there."

Tessa Hart, an employee whom Gabe had previously considered loyal, turned to him, trying not to laugh. "He's *your* brother."

Ah, yes, his brother. More like the worm in his tequila, the backwash in his beer, the sediment in his wine. And that was being kind. "I don't want to claim him. Not really." There were three O'Sullivan brothers, but Gabe and Daniel were normal. Sean, not so much.

Tessa pointed an accusing finger at him. "You own this place. Do your job."

Thus he was shamed into performing his duty as owner

of Prime, the infamous Manhattan bar that had been in the O'Sullivan family for nearly eighty years. Nowadays, the wooden floors creaked when you walked across them, but they glistened from fresh polish. Three dark mahogany bars shaped to form a "U" around the room, a brass railing running underneath.

Rows of photographs covered the walls. Some famous mugs, some mugs not so famous. Front and center behind the main bar were the pictures of the last four noble generations of O'Sullivans. An O'Sullivan had poured for sitting Presidents, Mafia dons, Joe DiMaggio and Bob Dylan—and now, apparently, this fine establishment was serving as the No-Tell Motel for one Sean O'Sullivan.

Oh, how the mighty had fallen.

Gabe scanned the bar, wondering which nubile young thing Sean had torpedoed this time. Slowly it dawned on him exactly who was missing and he grinned. Okay, maybe Sean wasn't so bad. Unfortunately that didn't put the ladies' room back in business.

He took the old, narrow staircase down to the twin doors that marked the ladies' room and the men's room, then rapped once on the former, hard and authoritative.

"Open up. It's the police. According to regulation ten-forty-three of the NY City Code, lascivious conduct is forbidden in public places."

From beyond the door came Sean's voice, stuck in the throes of more passion than Gabe wanted to imagine. "This wasn't a public place until you stuck your yap in it, Officer. And by the way, there's no Regulation ten-forty-three. I know the law."

"Are you insulting one of New York's finest?"

"No, I'm insulting my baby brother. Now go away and spare your brother a good seven—ah, darling, that's perfect—make it fifteen minutes."

"We have paying customers who need to use the facilities."

There was a pointed silence, followed by more lurid groaning.

Gabe leaned against the door, making himself comfortable. "Did you tell her you were a lawyer, Sean? Because I don't know why the women keep falling for that one. I guess it's hard for a man in the sanitation industry to attract a certain class of woman, although you ended up married easy enough. Could have been the pregnancy, I suppose? How's Laura doing, by the way?"

Gabe waited, counted to three…and finally heard the low murmur of heated voices. Not heated enough, dammit. Who knew a woman with so much power in the health department would be so desperate? Didn't matter, Gabe could stoop even lower. "The clinic called. The test results were positive, but with proper medication and professional counseling, you'll be able to live a completely normal life."

Eventually Sean's voice sounded again, a little less steady this time. "Go away. And have pity on a man who's about to go onto his fourth tour of duty and won't see a woman again for the next—aahhh—nine months."

How any woman—especially a New York City health inspector—could mistake his brother for a soldier was out of the range of rational possibility. Yet for some reason, rationality, Sean and women never went together anyway. Gabe banged on the door.

Sean yelled back. "You're embarrassing the poor woman, Gabe. Be a gentleman and leave."

Gabe shook his head. "All right, but don't think I won't remember this," he threatened.

"Instead of worrying about me, why don't you worry about Tessa?"

So typical of Sean. Diverting attention from the matters at hand. Three-card monte with emotional overtones. Sadly Gabe was suckered into it, because Tessa had enough problems to worry about, and it would be hell if something else came up and bit her in the butt.

"What *about* Tessa?" he asked.

"Employees not coming to Dr. Phil? Tsk-tsk…"

"What *about* Tessa?" Gabe repeated, seriously considering busting the door down, but he'd only replaced it three months ago, and doors weren't cheap, especially the seven-feet tall, two-feet wide, custom-made kind.

"Give me another six minutes and I'll tell you the whole story, because it's obvious she's keeping secrets from you."

With a frustrated sigh, Gabe put an "out of order" sign on the ladies' room door and went back upstairs. Thursday nights lacked the chaos of the weekend, but when the Yankees were on television, the crowd skewed to beer and bets. Even some of the daytime regulars were there, as well. Judging by the happy faces, the Yankees were winning.

An embarrassingly short two minutes later Sean appeared at the top of the basement steps with a tall brunette wearing schoolmarm glasses. Sean lifted her hands to his lips—just like Sir Fucking Lancelot. Jeez.

"I take it we passed inspection?" asked Gabe, keeping his face purposefully bland. Not that he needed to worry. The health inspector shot Sean a punch-drunk smile. "With flying colors. Flying. Colors," she murmured, and Sean beamed, an already healthy ego getting supersized. Shit. Sometimes Gabe wanted to shoot his brother, but Sean had connections everywhere, and the bar had never failed a health inspection yet. Okay, Gabe would forgive him. Right now he was more concerned about Tessa anyway.

He shot her a quick mental-health-check glance. Everything looked normal. She was mixing drinks with her usual Hollywood flair, tossing glasses into the air, to the delight of her male customers. But when she listened to an order, Gabe noticed the telltale tugging on the lock of hair that fell in her face.

Tessa attracted trouble like rain on a busted umbrella, but

that didn't matter to Gabe. When his employees needed him, he was there. Especially for Tess.

TESSA KNEW A TRAIN wreck idea when she heard it, and this was definitely one. She shot Gabe her best mean-girl glare, the one she'd been practicing in the mirror for nearly all of her twenty-six years. All that practice didn't mean she was any good, but she had to keep trying.

"I am not moving in with you. You're my boss, among other things. And don't think you can make me say yes by flashing those earnest blue eyes in my direction, because I'm learning to say the word *no* to men. No. N.O. *Non. Nyet. Nein.* I can say it in Navajo. *Dooda.* See, I can say *no.*"

To make sure her point was not missed, she lit a flame over the flaming Jägerbomb shooter she was making, still working the mean-girl glare.

Gabe hefted a bucket of ice into the bin, biceps rippling with the effort. The world's most perfect bartender. Understanding, thoughtful and sexy as hell.

"It's not like that, Tess," he said, flashing those earnest blue eyes in her direction. Four women sighed as they watched him work. Gawd, it was like synchronized lusting.

Tessa pulled a draft beer, then slid it down the bar to the waiting customer. In her heart she knew Gabe meant well. Gabriel O'Sullivan was more than just any bartender. He was the lifeline who'd given her a job when she'd shown up in Manhattan after a bitter breakup—because, after all, everyone knows that the brainiac thing to do after leaving all your worldly possessions in Florida with your old boyfriend is to move to stratospherically expensive New York with only a high school diploma and an encyclopedic knowledge of tropical bar drinks.

Not once had Gabe laughed at her, and for that, he earned her undying loyalty. Except that didn't mean she was moving in with him. On that she was standing firm. Firmish. Unfortunately she only had five days to find an apartment.

"You need a place to live," he continued, completely ignoring her denials. "I have an extra bedroom. It's the perfect solution."

"*I'm* looking for a place," answered one fake-blonde type with way too much eyeliner.

"Did you need a drink?" asked Tessa pointedly, absorbing the fake-blonde hate-vibes. The blonde would get over it, especially considering the way the suit behind her was eyeing her ass. Then Tessa turned her attention back to Gabe. "And don't you have a bar to cover? Look at poor Cain, he's in over his—" Tessa checked out the back bar, noticed Sean had ditched his usual jacket and tie and was working alongside Cain. Just once she should be right in her life. Just once. Was that too much to ask?

Four thirsty Con Ed workers lined the bar, and she mixed up four mojitos, grinding the mint leaves with a little more force than necessary. Abject pity usually did that to her.

"I'm helping you out here for a bit," he explained, right as the waitress, Lindy, came up with a whole barful of drink orders, leaving no space for idle chatter.

"Meyer's," called Gabe.

"Heads up," answered Tessa, tossing the bottle in his direction. Gabe flipped the bottle behind his back, then poured the rum into the glass, and before you could silently mouth the word *show-off,* he had blended up a beautifully constructed mai tai.

Tessa, never one to be outblended, scowled and threw the shot glass in the air, sending it spinning four revolutions with an extra half twist for good measure. The Con Ed guys applauded with gusto. Tessa beamed pointedly at Gabe. Yes, she was capable. A miracle-working mixologist. A miracle-working mixologist who was about to be homeless.

Some miracle.

Unless she agreed to Gabe's offer.

Sensing her momentary weakness, he leaned over her station and smiled in a manner guaranteed to break hearts and insure a fifty percent gratuity. "You need a place to live, Tessa. You can't live on the street."

Yeah, make her sound like a bag lady already. Tessa pushed bedraggled hair back from her face and met his eyes with dignity. Faked, but dignity nonetheless. Tessa was nothing if not proud.

"I could be some wet kitten or stray dog tossed out on the street by their heartless owner and you'd take me in. You're too soft. I know you, Gabriel O'Sullivan."

"You're not a stray dog."

"Thank you for that compliment."

"Come on, Tess. It makes sense."

She didn't need this conversation right now, but fine, if he wanted to explore the myriad reasons why she couldn't move in with him, she would list them off one by one. Starting with the obvious.

"You are a man."

He didn't roll his eyes, but he might as well have. "Yes."

Gabe pushed it off so easily, as if his physical attributes were no big deal. But that was what made him so irresistible. Dark brown hair that had a tendency to curl into the nape of his neck, blue eyes that crinkled at the edges, not too tall, not too short, not too bulky, not too lean and a full mouth that was curved into a perpetual smile. He called himself average—and compared to the potent animal magnetism of Sean, he was—but damn if the women didn't throw themselves all over that simple charm. Oh, yeah, he knew exactly what he did to the female species.

Tessa gave him a skeptical look. "I am a woman."

He handed Lindy three cosmopolitans without even breaking a sweat. "There is that."

"We cannot live together in blissful, platonic harmony.

It's impossible." Tessa had lived with a colorful menagerie of roommates, all female. And maybe she could have considered a lesser male as a roommate…but Gabe? No. That was just inviting trouble to come on in for a late-night drink.

Sean angled in front of her, fixing his place near a beautifully dressed brunette.

"I thought you were working," said Gabe.

"I was doing you a favor, but I got the phone number I wanted and now I'm no longer working. Now I'm just shooting the shit with my family and friends and listening to this fascinating conversation on the intricacies of the human libido. A male and a female living together is a huge mistake."

Gabe shook up a vodka martini. "With Tessa? I'm not worried."

Tessa coughed, the emotional equivalent of a furball stuck in her throat. "I don't know why I put up with this place."

Gabe flashed her an easy grin, and for one second the resemblance between Gabe and Sean was unmissable. Sean was broader, beefier, swore like a sailor, with a nose that had been broken in two bar fights since she'd known him, but somehow he was always impeccably dressed in a suit and tie.

"You put up with us because we like you and you're the fastest mojito maker on the Atlantic seaboard," said Gabe. "Sean, tell her she should move in with me."

Sean rested his chin on his palm. "Why should I contribute to what will be the loss of our finest frozen drink maker and chief barback when Tony doesn't show? Do I look like a moron? Oh, no, Gabe. This is all about me. I like Tess. I want her to stay gainfully employed at this fine establishment so I can flirt with the female patrons while she works her little ass off, finely shaped as it is. She moves in with you, and you two will be all over each other. Groping, fondling…" Sean illustrated with graphic hand movements. "I'd put good money on that one."

Tessa strategically avoided looking at Gabe. "I should sue you both. Male chauvinist perverts."

"Come on, Tess," Gabe insisted. "You know it's the perfect solution. We'll make it temporary."

"Temporarily forget about having sex then," added Sean. "With Tessa Trueheart here as your roommate, you can kiss that goodbye. One more reason this is a bad idea."

Sean was only half-right, and Tessa corrected the attack on her character. "I would never interfere in my roommate's personal activities. Hailey—the roommate before Janice—she had three boyfriends and none of them knew about the others, except for me, of course. I hated it. All that lying and pretending." She stuck out her tongue. "Blah."

Sean's expression sharpened, transforming into full *Law & Order* mode. "So you come home and Gabe here is getting busy with some fine young thing on the sofa. What do you do?"

"What time is it?" asked Tessa, pouring a Jack neat for a Wall Street type with kind eyes.

"What does that matter?" asked Gabe.

"It's important. If it's still daylight, and under civilized society's strictures for productivity—i.e. time for Tessa to hit the books—then I don't care who's doing it in my living area. I'm going to study or else I'll never get my degree."

"That's cold."

"You haven't lived with the number of roommates that I have. You have to have rules and order or you'll go crazy. You both are on your own. Someday soon I'm going to be on my own."

Tessa ended with a sigh, picturing herself walking up the mighty stone steps of her most prized apartment building, waving at Rodney the doorman before trudging into the old, quaint gated elevator that shuddered when it passed the third floor. After she made it safely upstairs, she'd open her door to solitary paradise, where she could crank up her Cher CD—

the one she hid from the world—and then she'd fall into a neatly covered periwinkle-blue chintz chair. A huge tabby cat would jump into her lap and curl up in the afternoon sun, purring like a vibrator—the one that she'd buy if she lived alone.

There were a lot of advantages to living life alone. Most people took it for granted. Tessa, who had always had someone breathing down her neck—and finishing off the last of the milk, craved it the way some women craved pricey shoes. And at Hudson Towers, not only would she have the apartment she wanted but she could afford the rent on a one-bedroom all on her own. Well, not right at this exact moment but very, very soon. Her savings were piling up nicely, and once she finished her associate's degree in finance—approximately forty-six more credit hours—she'd be good to go.

Gabe pulled out a bottle of Grey Goose and poured a shot. "Well, right now you need a roommate, and I think you should bunk with me until you find someone who isn't going to desert you again."

She shook her head. "Must you try and rescue every female you meet?"

"Yes, he must," answered Sean and then promptly stuck a celery stick into his mouth.

"At least think about it," Gabe said. "And if you're thinking about bunking in the storeroom until your find a place, think again, Tessa. It's against the law."

"In what state?"

"In my state. My bar. My state. My rules."

Tessa shot a lime wedge in his direction, not that it mattered. The writing was pretty much on the wall. With five days left before she had to move, she really didn't have much choice.

ALL NIGHT GABE POURED drinks, a gazillion cosmopolitans for a gazillion females who were all looking to meet Mr. Right or Mr. Wrong and the gazillion single males who skimmed in their wake. Yeah, it was a rough life. Actually, it was the only life he'd ever dreamed of. Gabe's great-grandfather had done it right.

In 1929, O'Sullivans had been a speakeasy when his great-grandfather fell dead at the age of fifty-three. Surprisingly enough, his wife had taken over, and ran the place until gin was flowing legally in New York again.

Years had passed and generations of O'Sullivans had worked the old bar. Each generation had taken it over and then spent their lives working to keep the place going. During World War II, Gabe's grandmother had split the bar into two real estate parcels, keeping one, and selling the other, which had been, up until a few months ago, a bodega. Gabe's father, Thomas O'Sullivan, had ignored the family business and chose to be a newspaperman until he died of a heart attack at fifty-six.

Gabe had inherited his great-grandfather's dream, a dream passed down to his grandfather, his uncle and finally Gabe. As a kid, he'd worked behind the bar illegally, which had only made it sweeter. He loved listening to people talk, loved meeting new people and in general loved the bar. Where else could a kid have his picture taken with the New York Yankees and the Teflon Don? Nowhere else but O'Sullivans.

After his uncle had died, Gabe had worked four jobs to pay the back taxes on the place to keep it open, and even then he'd needed his brothers' financial help. But things had worked out, and voilà, here he was. He'd updated the interior, changed the name from O'Sullivans to Prime and now he was mixing Jell-O shots with seven adoring females eagerly waiting on line to pay him for a drink, tip him another twenty and then scribble their phone numbers on the cocktail napkins. And the next step in the Gabe O'Sullivan hospitality empire? The full restoration of the bar into the space next door.

Considering the medical history of the male O'Sullivan genes, Gabe figured he didn't have any time to waste.

He winked at a particularly lovely specimen with coal-black hair and honey-colored eyes that dripped with the promise of a good time. Jasmine, he thought, and slid a glass of wine in front of her. "You're looking lovely tonight. Why aren't there five guys angling to buy you a drink?" It wasn't the most creative line in the world, but he wasn't looking to pick her up, he only wanted her to like his bar.

Tessa walked behind him and slapped him on the butt, and he didn't even stop as he reached for a clean glass. "Don't mind her. She's madly in love, but I keep telling her no."

Tessa muttered something incomprehensible but most likely insulting and then went back to work on the other side.

Eventually Jasmine moved on, to be replaced by Cosmopolitan Amy, Banana Daiquiri Lauren, Kamikaze Rachel, Cosmopolitan Vicki and, for one short moment, Wild Turkey Todd. The hours flew by, as they always did on a busy night, and Gabe never broke a sweat.

There were a few interventions, just as there always were. Two fake IDs, one male patron who decided that Lindy needed to show more cleavage and a couple of Red Sox fans who didn't understand that when in Yankees territory you better keep your mouth shut or get doused in beer. Typical but never boring.

Eventually the clock struck midnight and the crowds thinned to something less than chaos. Out of the corner of his eye Gabe noticed Cain handing Seth a twenty at the back bar, which meant only one thing. There was a new bar pool on the bulletin board downstairs.

Gabe took the stairs to the basement, where the kitchen/office/storage/bathrooms were located, as well as the betting board. Sure enough, a white sheet of paper was tacked up with a grid of numbers and letters. Nothing to indicate the bet, though. When would they learn the right way to run a pool? Amateurs.

While he was enjoying the calm, Gabe began breaking down beer cases, and soon Cain was downstairs, adding a new square to the grid. Cain was quiet and bulky, a New York fireman who bartended on the weekend in order to survive. You'd think they'd pay men better to risk their lives by running into burning buildings, but no. Gabe didn't mind, because he judged every man by how fast he could mix a martini, and Cain was almost as good as Tessa. Almost.

"What's the bet?" Gabe asked.

"You don't want to know," said Cain loading a rack of glasses through the dishwasher.

"Yeah, I do."

"It was all Sean's idea."

Which wasn't encouraging. "What's the bet?"

"How long you and Tessa can last."

"As roommates?"

"Before you have sex."

Gabe felt a punch in his head not unlike being clocked with a two-by-four. "You're joking with me, right?"

Cain looked at him blandly. "No. Want to put some money down?"

Gabe swallowed. There were women that Gabe had sex with and women Gabe didn't have sex with. In his head, Gabe had long ago covered Tessa's body with a habit and a veil and pushed any sort of sweaty, thrusting thoughts far, far away. She'd come to New York still wearing the scars from her last relationship. In four years you'd think she'd have recovered—but, no, you'd be wrong. Tessa wasn't like other women. She had her own set of goals, her own strange focus in life, and men weren't a part of it, which was why she was the only woman he'd ever consider as a roommate, and only because of said habit and veil. When you lived with Mother Teresa, it wasn't hard to keep things platonic.

However, right now it was past midnight and Gabe had been

the recipient of four pairs of panties, seventeen phone numbers and assorted sexual propositions and, okay, he was a little wired.

It always happened as the night wore on. No big deal.

Gabe mentally clothed Tessa back in the habit, ordered his hard-on back in the bag, and pasted an easy smile on his face.

"You guys didn't say anything to Tessa, did you?"

"You're kidding, right? She put down a bet."

Oh, God. The habit and veil were slowly being peeled away, but Gabe kept that damned smile on his face. "Poor kid, I'll have to let her down easy. How long did she think she'd last?"

"Hell Freezes Over. Last entry, right here." Cain pointed to the board where HFO was neatly penned in black ink.

"She said that?"

"Her exact words weren't ambiguous, but you got a fragile ego. So you gonna bet? The pot's almost three grand."

Gabe continued to break down boxes with an amazing amount of compressed energy. "I won't encourage morally bankrupt games of chance in my bar."

"What about the Super Bowl pool, March Madness, the Subway series and last month's bet on which patron was most likely to get breast enhancements?"

That one lapse in judgment had cost Gabe a sweet thousand dollars. And who knew that the Yankees would actually choke in the bottom of the ninth? "Shut up, Cain."

"I have to go upstairs. Lindy can't cover the bars alone."

"Tessa's gone? I wanted to talk to her before she went home."

Cain shrugged. "Her shift was over. She left. If you run, you could probably catch her before she hits the subway station."

Gabe bit back a curse and headed out into the long, lonely darkness that was Manhattan at the midnight hour. The outside air was cool and crisp and felt marvelous after being cooped up in the bar for so long. He broke into a run simply because he needed to move.

Around the corner and down two flights of stairs was the

station, occupied by the usual patrons. A group of late-night partygoers trying to find their way back to Jersey. A mediocre saxophone player blowing out what was supposed to be the blues. A few kids heading home. A set of foreign tourists taking pictures. And, yes, there was Tessa, standing alone, waiting for the train.

"Why do you always do this? You know that one of us is supposed to walk you down here."

"I haven't needed supervision after dark since Giuliani was mayor, Gabe. Besides, I got my mace. They know not to mess with me."

"Still."

"What are you really here for?" she asked him quite patiently. That was Tessa. Never out of sorts. His gaze skimmed over her, checking for some sort of weakness, but there wasn't any, which for some reason always surprised him.

Not that she was hard. Oh, no, Tessa was all cotton and smiles, but she held herself back, one step between her and the rest of the male world. Gabe included.

However, there was something oddly vulnerable about the whacked brown hair that had never seen a decent cut juxtaposed against the model-sharp cheekbones that could cut glass. Like a painting half-done or a bridge half-built.

A work in progress. That was Tessa, too.

Her summer-green eyes look tired, but she was bouncing back and forth on the soles of her running shoes, still full of energy, going home to an apartment that would be gone in five days.

"I wanted to hammer out the details before you went home. I got Danny to cover for me all day on Monday, so I think we're good to go." He was actually there to see if the bet had unsettled her, but she didn't look worried. So if she wasn't worried, then he wasn't worried either.

"You know this is only temporary."

"As long as you need. I don't use the room much anyway. I can put everything in storage tomorrow."

"Don't you dare touch a thing. I won't take up any space. Besides, this is short-term. Temporary, just like you said. I'm not going to cramp your style. It's all about education for me, Gabe. I've got a few notices posted around the campus, and on craigslist, so hopefully something will pop soon and I'll be out of your hair. Three weeks tops."

"It doesn't matter how long you stay. You know that."

"Yes, I do know that, and you're a sweet man, but I need to take care of myself."

"I'm really not a sweet man, you know."

"You gonna make me move in all by myself, Mr. Un-sweetened Man?"

Gabe stuck his hands in his pockets. "How much furniture do you have?"

"A twin bed, a nightstand and some books," she answered, with a remarkably sweet smile.

"Oh, yeah, that'll take seven minutes to load up. I'll borrow the truck from Cain and be there at ten."

The lights of the train appeared in the tunnel and she stood on tiptoe, planting a friendly kiss on his cheek, "You really are a sweet man."

"I'm not a sweet man."

Tessa pointed up the tracks. "Look, that old lady—she's getting mugged!"

Gabe took off running, but Tessa's laughter stopped him in midstride.

"Busted!"

He walked back, whapped her on the arm. "I was going to clean up the place for you, but not anymore."

The doors on the train slid open, and she waved before slipping inside.

Gabe didn't bother to wave back. *Sweet man, my ass.*

2

MOVING DAY WAS A piece of cake. Of course, that's the way of it when all your worldly possessions fit into three wooden packing crates. Except for the decrepit twin bed, which Gabe glared at, nostrils flaring in disdain—not a usual look for him. She didn't like his judging her possessions—or lack thereof—and so Tessa protested a few minutes longer than she might have if he had remained glareless.

Janice, her former roommate, had already moved out, and the apartment was depressingly barren. Tessa ignored the equally depressing sensation in her gut. Moving in was always a new adventure. Moving out was another change-of-address form and another adventure squandered.

For once, Tessa wanted to know that when she changed her address it was because of something good, something positive, something that Tessa could be proud of.

Gabe, not sensing Tessa's emotional turmoil (typical male), hovered over the thin metal frame and then poked a finger at the mattress. "This is your bed?"

It was stupid to get worked up over a mattress that belonged in a Dumpster, but seeing Gabe mentally inventorying her life reminded her of how far she still had to go.

"A featherweight mattress is easier to move." She slung it over one shoulder to demonstrate. "See?"

He stood firm. "That's not going into my place."

"This is my bed. What am I supposed to sleep on?"

Gently Gabe disentangled her fingers from their death grip on the mattress. "I'll buy you a futon."

"I hate those," she began and then stopped, sighed. There was no point in lying—she loved futons. "I don't want you buying me furniture. I can afford it." And she could. Her savings account was surprisingly healthy considering her lack of furniture and fashionable attire. Tessa had priorities—namely the perfect one-bedroom apartment in Hudson Towers.

And it was perfect. A prewar building on West End Avenue. With a board that kept out the riffraff, but wasn't crazy-stringent about it either. Reasonable rents and maintenance fees a full seven percent less than the average. They had redone the shared space four years ago, a great use of morning light and windows. The place had a part-time doorman, Rodney, which was much more sensible than hiring a full-time doorman who would only sit on his heinie all day and earn union wages from overpriced rents.

Ah, someday...

"You sure you can afford a bed?" Gabe asked, pulling her out of her apartment fantasies. She hadn't planned on buying a new bed, but her old one was on its last legs, literally. At her nod, he tossed the mattress in the corner.

After that, she picked up a crate and headed for the door. "First ground rule—no more making fun of Tessa's stuff. Observe the boundaries, we'll be fine."

He opened the door for her, politely following behind. "Deal. Now let's get you home."

GABE'S BUILDING WAS A postwar elevator building on the Upper East Side. The outside was a little too seventies for her own taste, but since he'd owned it for over ten years and it was probably worth close to seven figures, she figured she'd give him a break. That, and the cut-rate—i.e. free—rent. That had been another argument she had lost. However, as a consolation prize he'd let her buy lunch.

In the lobby there was a full-time doorman, Herb, a teapot of a man with a five-o'clock shadow on steroids. And once they got to Gabe's floor she noticed the nice view, without parking garages to block the sight of the East River.

All in all, the apartment was as she'd imagined. A legitimate two-bedroom, not one of those skimpy conversions from a large one-bedroom. The main living area had all the basic essentials: television, couch and a dining table, mostly covered with newspapers. The kitchen was galley-style and definitely not big enough for two. However, the appliances were a step above what she was used to.

"You can live here?" he asked while she examined it room by room.

Thoughtfully she walked around, keeping her face nonjudgmental, wanting to make him nervous. "Yup," she answered quietly.

He backed against the wall, far away from her—but not far enough. She was used to him at work, but this felt different. More intimate. If it hadn't been for that stupid bet, she wouldn't be nervous at all.

There was a silence, an awkward silence. A silence she normally would've filled, except she knew he would've seen through that because she wasn't a social chitchat gal. He folded his hands across his chest, not seemingly affected at all. Of course, he was used to silence. He was used to living alone.

He.

Gabe.

Tessa felt it again. That fast leap in her stomach, like flying downhill on the Cyclone. She shrugged it off. Life was full of ups and downs and screeching corners, and she wasn't about to let a little chronic stomach anxiety ruin anything.

This was temporary. She'd be out of his hair soon enough.

She put on a cocky smirk and looked around, anywhere but at him. "It's great. Listen, I should go study," she said and promptly fled the room.

FOUR HOURS LATER, SHE was already settled, sitting on her brand-new futon. The earlier flicker of fear had caught her by surprise. And it wasn't just any fear. No, it was the dreaded man-fear. The implications of living with Gabe had suddenly hit her in places where she didn't want to feel those complicated implications.

Denny had been the only man she had ever *lived* with, and in those young, naive days, he had convinced her that she didn't need to worry about her future. College? Nah. If she only hooked up with Denny Ericcson, then all her dreams would come true. So Tessa deferred the college years, took a part time job as a bartender and spent her days tanning on the sunny Florida beaches. But then her twenty-second birthday arrived. Denny told her that the relationship had gone stale and he was ready to move on, because he wasn't the one-woman-forever type. Putting her out to pasture at twenty-two.

Dreams could come true? Ha. More like nightmares.

Needless to say, the last four years had been manless. No hookups, no man dreams and, yes, there'd been times in the past when she'd felt momentary urges, but nothing lasting. As a bartender, it was expected that your customers would hit on you. You learned how to either brush aside the urges or act on them. Tessa was a brush-asider, always a brush-asider.

And, to be honest, she'd had urges for Gabe before, too, because, well, she wasn't blind, or stupid, and Gabe was...

Oh, God. Living with him was going to kill her study skills.

Even her room was filled with his presence, and he wasn't even here. She felt like an intruder in this place that was so obviously his.

A metal desk stood in the corner, covered with O'Sullivan family photos, papers nearly overflowing the top. A weight bench sat next to the window, and a monstrous collection of vinyl records sat in open boxes in the corner. Her first thought was to snoop, but that was a violation of all the roommate privacy regulations that she kept dear.

No, she was going to study, so Tessa covered her face with her accounting book, blocking out all temptation. Eventually the sinking fund method of depreciation brought her back to a mind-numbing cold reality. And then, as if to really drag her back to reality, her mother called.

"Hi, Mom," she said, abandoning all pretense of studying and wandering over to look at the O'Sullivan family pictures.

"How did you know it was me? Were you thinking of your favorite mother?"

"Caller ID, Mom." Her mom was a Luddite where technology was concerned, but Tessa forgave her for it.

"Your phone's been disconnected."

With a heavy and completely audible sigh, Tessa put back the photo of three dark-headed boys in Little League uniforms.

"I moved, Mom," she said, before mouthing the word *Again?*

"Again?"

Argh.

"Mom, you don't understand the Manhattan apartment market. Rents are always changing, fees are going up, rentals turn into co-ops overnight. You have to stay on your toes, ready to handle whatever comes your way."

"That assumes that someone can handle whatever comes their way."

"How long have I lived on my own?"

"You've been in New York for four years, but you never have lived on your own. You should come back to Florida, Tessa. Your family is here and we can help you."

Tessa returned to the comfort of her futon and leaned her

head against the wooden back. This was a horse that'd been beaten, eviscerated and then hung on the wall as modern art. "Thank you, Mom, but no. I love you, and Florida's grand, but I'm doing fine here. Honestly."

"I just worry. If something happens, who's going to take care of you? Are you eating okay?"

"Pastrami and rye for lunch."

"Getting enough sleep?"

"Oh, yeah," Tessa answered, stifling a yawn.

"How are the classes going?" Her mom had never approved of her going back for a degree, which meant only one thing: there was an ulterior motive to this conversation, and Tessa probably wasn't going to like it.

Time to transition from negative energy to something positive—like hanging up.

"Good. Listen, Mom, I have an accounting quiz this week and I need to study. Talk to you soon, 'bye."

Because she didn't like the idea of lying to her mom, she opened her accounting book and went after it again. However, her concentration was elsewhere, poking through the record collection, browsing the photos. In short, being everything she hated in a nosy person. So Tessa loaded up her book bag, stuck her feet into a pair of flip-flops and headed for the door.

Sacked out on the living room couch, sleeping peacefully, without a worry in the world, was the source of her wandering concentration. It must be marvelous to take a nap in the afternoon. Her lips curved into a smile as she watched him sleep. He'd been the one constant in her life since she'd moved to New York, but she'd never seen him sleep. His chest rose and fell as he breathed, one arm flung over the edge. He even snored a little, a comfortable rumble that was low and even. She'd have to tease him about that. A plaid throw dangled from one armrest, and she took it, tucking it around him.

Instantly the hazy blue eyes opened. "Problem?"

Tessa jumped back, caught red-headed in the act of intruding on his space. "Heading off to Starbucks."

Gabe didn't seem to notice her violation, instead rubbing at his forehead with two fingers. "Sounds great. Can you bring me back a cup?"

"I'm going to study and then I'm heading for class."

He sat up, tossing the throw aside, and Tessa took another step back. Wow, twelve hundred square feet could really be tiny at times.

"You can study here. Set up at the table or the desk in the back room. I can toss my stuff on the floor."

"I have trouble concentrating. It's a self-discipline tactic. When I go to the coffee shop, I know I'm there to study."

"Ha. Some people go for coffee. Unenlightened plebes."

She was about to launch into a lecture, but he held up a hand. "I know, I know. I won't interfere. Personal space. Sorry. This is new to me. What about dinner? I'm thinking either pasta or Thai."

"Don't worry about me. I'll grab a sandwich after class. And FYI, I'll be back around seven in case you want to get out, or, uh, have company or something."

His mouth twitched. "Sure."

TESSA'S ACCOUNTING CLASS was at the Knightsbridge Community College in Queens, which overlooked Flushing Bay. Forty people comprised her class. Young students, old students, an ethnic smorgasbord from all walks of life. Tessa had never doubted her abilities to breeze through this class with eyes closed, but...

Last week's test was the first item on the menu, and Professor Lewis walked up and down the aisles, handing out papers with a smile or a frown. When he reached Tessa, he frowned.

She frowned in return.

Her frown grew even darker when she saw the fat red D scrawled on the top of the test. This had to be a mistake, because a failing grade was not part of her life plan.

She waited patiently through the lecture, sneaking a peek at the paper every few minutes, checking to make sure she had read it correctly—maybe it was a half-assed B—but, no, with all the red circles, there was no mistake.

After the clock ticked the hour and her classmates started to file out, Tessa walked up to the prof's desk on slightly wobbly legs, reminding herself that she faced angry drunks at three in the morning. This shouldn't be a problem. Professor Lewis was long past middle age, with a thin, ruddy face that indicated a long love affair with, most likely, scotch.

"I wanted to talk to you about the test," said Tessa, giving him the opening to immediately correct her grade.

He gave a long look at the clock, as though he was ready to take off, and then started drumming his pencil eraser on the desk. *Too bad, buddy.*

"There's not much to say, Miss Hart. You stumbled over key concepts. Allowance for Doubtful Accounts and Inventory Flow, and you made a mess of the Statement of Changes in Financial Position. I was horribly disappointed in your work. Substandard. Are you sure you studied?"

"Didn't everyone do equally bad?" she asked, because she had spent three days going over formulas and she could feel her blood pressure elevating, possibly in anger but probably in pure ice-bitten anxiety.

"Actually, the average was quite high. Eighty-three."

Which meant no curve, which meant she still had a D. *Damn.* Her blood pressure notched up higher.

"Look, I don't think you understand," she said, trying to keep the quiver out of her voice. "I can't make a C in this class, much less a D. It's A or B all the way, because if I come out of community college with anything less than a three-point-oh, I'll be screwed at getting into anyplace else. And at this juncture in my life's journey I really need to be thinking beyond a two-year degree. I need a future. I need a career."

"I feel your pain."

Oh, I bet you do. Typical scotch drinker, always thinking of yourself.

"Can I make this up with extra credit? An assignment, a paper, something, anything?"

"Study hard for the final, Miss Hart. That'll clean your grade up nicely."

Tessa shoved the paper low in her book bag. "Thanks," she murmured through clenched teeth and headed outside.

COLLEGE WAS NOT supposed to be this hard. She had aced high school, graduated with honors. This was college. A community college. Not even a four-year program. Everyone had told her that it'd be easy. Sean had told her she would finish with flying colors—summa cumma whoma. So why was she having problems?

Tessa considered going back to Gabe's place, but she wasn't in full control yet. The test was burning a hole in her bag. She was going to have to convince him that everything was peachy. So she did what she always did when she wanted to regain control: she took the Manhattan apartment tour.

She started by heading south down Fifth Avenue, the setting sun glinting on the windows. Her favorite building was the San Remo, with the two white finial-topped towers that stood guard over Central Park. The building was all 1930s art deco and class, the grand dame of co-ops in the city. Old, with a history that was older than Carnegie.

The board was rumored to be less fussy than the one at the Dakota, but they had ixnayed Madonna as a tenant back in the eighties, so they did have some minimal standards. There was a full-time doorman, a plethora of classic six and seven floor plans and a stunning limestone cartouche that rose above the entrance like a magnificent eagle.

Two blocks south was the Dakota, "the" address in New York. People who lived here were looking for an address, a destination in life. Personally Tessa thought it was overrated because the old building looked like a medieval prison instead of a home. There was no personality, only accoutrements out the wazoo. By the time the sun had quit the day, she had walked past the Beresford, 740 Central Park West and the Ardsley. These were the apartment buildings that defied gravity in the real-estate market.

The buildings weren't for her—they didn't have the simple charm of Hudson Towers—but they were symbols of the resolution of the city. The roots that had been laid down so long ago, that no man would ever put asunder. Staring at the limestone facades that had seen so many years, so many changes, Tessa felt the calm return.

She was here. She would make it.

She would survive.

It was time to go home. As she was entering Gabe's building, her cell rang again. This time it was her brother, Robert.

Now Tessa was starting to get suspicious, so she took the call from a chair in the lobby. Yes, her family could be overly protective at times, but they weren't overly chatty.

"Why are you calling a mere three hours after our mother?"

"No reason. Just wanted to see how you were doing."

"I'm fine. Why shouldn't I be fine, Robert? Why do you think I shouldn't be fine?"

"Can't I call my sister to see what's up?"

"No, because you don't like to talk. You're uncommunicative—unless it's an emergency. Why is this an emergency?"

She heard the long sigh, which meant she was getting closer. "It's nothing."

"Tell me exactly what nothing is."

"Fine. It's Denny."

Denny. Ex-live-in-boyfriend Denny. No big deal.

"His girlfriend's pregnant. They're going to get married."

And now ex-live-in-boyfriend Denny was going to be Daddy Denny. No problem that he hadn't wanted a ball and chain or kids four years ago. But now? Oh, now his sperm was flying all over the planet, happily procreating at will.

"That's great," Tessa said, knowing that he expected her to say something—or else fall apart.

"You're taking this well."

"Of course I'm taking this well. It was four years ago, Robert. Time heals all wounds, and my wounds are closed, scars are faded. I'm getting on with my life. Did Mom tell you that I moved today? It's a great place. Two-bedroom. Doorman. Nice location on the Upper East Side. I haven't lived here before, never really thought I was upper east side material, but I think I'm going to like it." She was rambling now, but Robert wouldn't know any better.

"Okay, then. We were worried."

"About me? Pshaw. Stop worrying," she said and hung up before her face splintered into a million pieces.

For the last four years she had kept her focus on one thing only—supporting herself. She didn't have time for men or relationships, it wasn't in her plan. And off in Florida—happy, carefree Florida—there was Denny, who was having tons of sex with women, happily supporting himself and now a new wife and kid.

It sucked.

She waved happily to Herb as she boarded the elevator and was tempted to go out alone somewhere, anywhere, to have a good time, to see what she'd been missing, but she was tired, she wanted to lie down and she needed to climb into her bed and possibly never come out again.

At the apartment, Gabe was nursing a beer and watching

the Yankees win. The all-American singleton life. A man who didn't have to worry about accounting tests or failed relationships and in general treated life as if it were a soufflé to be whipped into shape.

"How was class?"

"Great," she answered and trotted to her room where she closed the door and collapsed.

She wasn't going to cry, because crying was for people who were lost or homeless or lived alone. When you had roommates, you learned to suffer in silence, listening to the awful pounding of your heart, knowing the tears hovered close to the surface but you had to master them and control them. She took out her accounting book, but the tears started to spill onto the pages, and a water-damaged textbook certainly wasn't going to help her grade.

She hated Denny Ericcson with a passion. Hated him for letting her think that her life was taken care of for forever and then ripping the rug right out from under her a mere three years after the fact. She peeled away the waistband of her jeans and saw the permanent proof of her idiocy: a tattoo on her butt. D-E-N-N-Y inked in cute red letters with a curlicue at the end.

Argh.

Instead of celebrating their third year together, she'd ended up starting all over. It was a time when most women had their lives all mapped out. Tessa wiped her face. She wasn't going to give him the satisfaction of tears. Not anymore. Of course, no way was she going to face her roommate, her cheeks warm and no doubt stained rosy-red.

She crept along the soft carpet of the hallway, soundlessly heading for the safety of the bathroom. Tessa looked up, met Gabe's eyes and then made a clean run for the lavatory, slamming the door behind her.

3

Gabe's first instinct was to hammer on the door and ask what was wrong. Tessa wasn't a crier, wasn't the emotional whirlpool that the other females at the bar were. Time after time he saw her move from place to place, moving from day job to job or whatever life threw at her, and she took it all in stride. There was only one other person he knew who was so emotionally stable. Him. No, Tessa was solid rock all the way. Which was why he'd been so shocked to see her upset.

However, Tessa had been very clear about things. The first being the ground rules. She wanted her space, and he'd been fine with that, although that was before she'd turned on the waterworks, and tears always got him hinky.

He crumpled the beer can in his hand, then tossed it in the trash across the room.

Damn.

Damn, damn, damn.

He didn't give a damn about the personal boundaries at the moment, so he went and knocked on the door. Loudly, so she wouldn't pretend not to hear, which is what he knew she'd do.

"Tess? I'm getting kinda bored out here. Let's go out, get some drinks. You know, celebrate your first night here."

"Go away, Gabe. It's that time of the month."

Aw, hell. When females freely admitted to PMS it meant serious danger ahead. He knocked again.

"Leave me alone, Gabe."

"I know you have your rules, Tess, but at least talk to me."

"No."

Gabe fought the urge to pound on the door, but now wasn't the time to be heavy-handed and go all caveman on her. He needed to use finesse and psychology. He was good at that, he was a bartender, a very good one. There was one easy way to get to Tess.

"Can you open the door? It is mine, after all."

The door opened and Tessa flew out. He grabbed her arm before she could run.

"Stop it."

She faced him down, every trace of a tear scrubbed away, her eyes sharp as daggers. All nice and neat and as tidy as she could get.

"I won't pry. I won't ask what's bothering you. However, I will treat you exactly like I'd treat any other friend who's had a hard day. There's a party upstairs. I'm a popular guy— sorry, you'll have to get used to that, but we should go. You'll get a chance to meet some of the people in the building, but watch out for Stevie Tagglioli—he's a basket case and will hit on anything in a skirt."

Tessa pulled her arm free and stared at the wall. "I don't feel like doing anything. I need to study."

So this was going to be tricky. She was playing the academic-scholar card. But there was one thing that trumped academics: guilt. "You're going to be boring, aren't you? I thought this would be fun. Somebody to eat with, hang out on the couch with, go shoot some pool—but, no, you're a closet dweeb, aren't you?"

She lifted her tiny chin, her eyes starting to spark. "I'm not a dweeb, and you'll be wise to remember that in the future."

"Prove it. Come on, it'll be fun."

"It's going to be hell."

"So we dip into the bowels of hell together? Besides, there's this one girl in the building—Vanessa—and she's been hitting on me, can't get enough of me. You can be my cover date."

And *voilà*. There it was. Fire-breathing rage. This was the Tessa that he knew and loved.

"You want me to keep some skank from hitting on you? *This* is the sole reason you're inviting me?"

"Does there have to be another one?"

Her eyes narrowed suspiciously. "This won't work. Now we're living together. If people in the building think we're a couple, what happens if I want to date someone in the building? Do I have to sneak out on you? See what sort of tangled webs evolve when you keep the skanks at bay with false pretense?"

Okay, she had him, but at least, she was smiling and contemplating the social world again. Progress. Definite progress. Gabe mentally congratulated himself.

"Does that mean you'll go?"

"No."

"You can't spend all your time locked in your room. You should get out and have some fun."

"I don't have time for fun."

"Everyone has time for fun."

"Oh, yeah, *everyone* has time for fun," she said, her eyes sharpening, her voice snapping, and Gabe wasn't sure exactly who "everyone" was, but he was definitely glad that it wasn't him, because judging by the daggers in her eyes, Tessa Hart was nursing a grudge the size of Brooklyn.

"It's exactly what you need. Take a break. Let yourself go for a night. You get too focused sometimes, Tess, and you miss out."

"You think I miss out?"

"On lots," he said, no longer sure what they were talking about, but she wasn't mad anymore, she wasn't sad anymore, and that was progress.

She twisted a lock of hair in her fingers. "There'll be people there? Fun people?"

"Yeah, tons."

Her eyes sparked. "I think you're right. It's time to move forward, and a party with fun people is the perfect way to start."

Ah, success. It was a sweet thing. Gabe gave her a friendly smile and watched as she went to get changed, the bounce back in her step.

It was a mere ten minutes later when she emerged from her room decked out in a miniskirt, a sheer blouse over a camisole and heels.

He looked once. He looked twice, and then his vision started to blur. Mother Teresa had left the building, and the woman that was left was…Tessa.

His roommate.

Small, supple and increasingly bedable.

Aw, no.

From out of the dregs of his imagination burst pictures and, even worse, full-motion videos. And from those images burst forth a hard-on that was excruciatingly painful—and it wasn't even nine o'clock.

"What do you think?" she asked.

"Good," he answered, because if he told her what he really thought, he was absolutely sure some personal boundaries would be violated.

He was used to her in jeans, a Prime T-shirt, and an absence of makeup. But, gawd, tonight she was smokin' and ready for anything. There was a do-me flicker in her eyes that threatened to knock him flat on his ass.

Gabe nodded stupidly and went to guide her toward the door, but that would involve touching her. He knew—even crazed and unthinking as he currently was—that was a bad idea. His hand dropped and he waited for her to open the apartment door.

A drop of sweat beaded on the back of his neck.

Hell.

THE PARTY WAS ON the thirty-seventh floor, hosted by one Jonathan Wilder, who worked in advertising sales and seemed to know the world. The apartment was packed and loud, and Gabe could see Tessa's eyes light up like a slot machine when she entered.

Trouble, and he spotted it right off the bat. He knew Tessa. He knew that tilt in her chin, that kick in her walk. When she got like that at the bar, a drink would end up right over some jerk's head.

Those sorts of safe and familiar thoughts pulled him back into a place where his Johnson didn't hurt quite so much and where that skirt didn't look quite so…easy.

Okay, he'd play bouncer tonight. He knew that role. He'd watch her back—not her ass, only her back—and keep her out of trouble.

However, tonight trouble was her middle name. She launched into a tequila shot contest with Stevie Tagglioli, and Gabe waited, thinking she was going to splash some tequila all over Stevie, but she didn't. She kept drinking…and touching…and drinking…and there was more touching. Eventually Gabe insinuated himself between the two, accidentally elbowing Stevie in the gut.

"Hey, Steve? Meet my new roommate, Tessa Hart."

"We're not involved," said Tessa, downing another shot.

Gabe laughed. "She's such a tease. Come on, babe. Let's move along while you can still walk."

Little Stevie was enthralled, spending more time staring at the thin silk of her shirt rather than her face. *Prick.*

Tessa's fingers bit into Gabe's arm. "Leave me alone," she huffed.

"You're in a mood, and I don't know why, and you don't have to tell me why because you want your space, but if you do something that you'll regret with somebody in this building that you're going to see every day, then you're going to experience history's longest hangover."

She pulled him aside, her eyes lit with some weird fire, ready to combust. "I'm merely trying to have some fun. Isn't that what you said? It'll be fun? I think that's an exact quote. Well maybe I *want* to have some fun."

She was mad at *him?*

Gabe swore and let go of her arm as if it burned. He couldn't reason with her, he wasn't going to try. "Fine. Your life. Your mistake."

And so it went on. Gabe watched from the sidelines, glaring when the females approached him. Tessa was the only one that drew his eyes. She drank shots, she flirted with every single male in the room—not one man left unflirted with, except for Gabe, of course, because she was shooting him death stares every few minutes. He stood, waiting for the crash, but that would be a long time coming because, truly, there were few people who could drink Gabe under the table, but Tessa was one. She had the tolerance of a T. rex. In fact, when faced with the mighty beast, she'd probably drink Godzilla under the table, too.

So he watched her, silently seething, seeing a completely new side to this woman. She'd pulled her hair back, exposing those killer cheekbones and a long, slender neck, and she'd put on red lipstick. Hooker-red lipstick—which, of course, looked like sex. *Goddamn.*

He didn't want to notice the full, red, glistening lips, didn't want to notice how long her legs were in heels, didn't want to notice how her nipples stood at attention under the flimsy silk, but she'd been right earlier.

It was hell. His mood got more foul, his cock got more hard, and when she started dancing on the coffee table, Gabe was pretty much at the end of his rope.

"We're going—now," he said, watching her hips sway, like a hypnotizing cobra, twisting, begging him to follow.

"Go home, Gabe," she said, raising her arms up over her head. A goddess reaching for the heavens, which only angered him even more because, dammit, he did not think poetry.

"Without you? No. This isn't like you, Tess."

That stopped the sway of her hips. *Thank you, God.*

"How do you know? Do you know the real me?"

"Yes," he replied, lifting her down. His hands lingered for a moment too long, but she didn't notice.

"Maybe I've changed."

"Not over the period of four hours." He grabbed her hand and pulled. She pulled back.

"I want to stay with Stevie."

And that was it. Gabe didn't care anymore. Stevie was the world's biggest jerk and loser, and once he got his fangs into Tessa, he wouldn't let go. Gabe picked up Tessa and threw her over his shoulder. She'd be furious, but she'd thank him in the morning.

The nasty jab between the shoulder blades indicated otherwise, but Gabe didn't even blink. He was willing to earn a purple heart for this one.

"Sorry. We had a bad fight. Go on, ignore us. Get some more of that spinach dip. It's really good," Gabe said encouragingly, shouldering his way through the crowd with Tessa beating on his back.

She didn't seem to remember that Gabe was used to dealing with drunk and disorderlies. But then, Gabe didn't usually cup their asses in such a familiar manner, either.

"Put me down, Gabe O'Sullivan."

"When I get you home, Miss Hart, and not before."

He almost let her down in the elevator, but she tried to run, so he hefted her back on his shoulder. God, the woman needed to gain weight.

"Gabe, I really hate you for this."

"In the morning, if you still hate me—which is a big *if*—

I'll apologize. You'll probably be thanking me, and I'll let you grovel in gratitude for a while, but right now you've had too much to drink—"

"I'm not drunk."

"Then it's even worse, Tess. Are you going to tell me what happened?"

"No."

"Fine."

"Fine."

The doors opened, and she slid down his body, slow and seductive. She probably didn't mean it to be that way, but his cock jumped just the same. Tessa shot him a look—not an invitation but coy and aware.

She knew.

So maybe it was time to stop playing games. Gabe trapped her outside the elevator against the wall, her lean body tight to his. He could feel every inch of her. The fluttering pulse, the tight nipples, the soft hips. She drew in a breath, soft and shaky, and the air burned. His hands itched to go lower, to explore and discover this new and marvelously arousing Tessa. But Gabe was still hanging on to the last edges of his control. His body wasn't happy, but his body would get over it.

"Inside. Now," he said, unlocking his apartment door. This time she didn't argue and went inside, but he knew from the tight set of her shoulders that she wasn't happy either.

Once in the apartment, he shut the door with a bang and ran a frustrated hand through his hair.

"It's late," he said because he needed to be alone. Needed to have her out of his sight. He needed to reclaim the image of Tessa from before. Hopefully it was still there, embedded somewhere deep in his brain.

"I'm not a kid," she answered, pushing her hair back from her face, and—God help him—gawky and angular had turned exotic.

"Then stop acting like one," he snapped, not leaving her alone as he had planned.

"You're not my father," she blurted, hands on hips—lean hips that he could still feel against his chest.

"I'm your friend, your boss and currently your roommate," he answered, mainly to remind himself of those key facts.

She walked toward the dining room table, away from the sensible safety of her bedroom. His gaze locked on her hips, tracking the sway with lethal intent. Stupidly he followed after her.

"Some friend, Gabe. I bet you wouldn't do this if Cain was hitting on some woman."

"No, Cain outweighs me by fifty pounds." Humor—another excellent way to defuse tense situations. He could feel the sweat on his brow, the rapid pulse vibrating under his skin. He stood frozen, needing her to break into a grin, or whap him on the arm.

But the room fell eerily quiet, and he waited, watching the rise and fall of her breasts, not moving, just waiting.

Eventually she moved, her breath coming out in a rush, and she came toward him, jamming a finger into his chest, which was completely the wrong thing to do. Completely. She shouldn't touch him. Not now.

"Do you want to know what's bothering me? I haven't had sex in four years. Tonight I wanted to have sex."

Four years? His already pained heart stopped completely, before kicking in again. He shouldn't have been happy about this bit of information, but his cock was.

Oh, it was thrilled.

"You want to have sex? Good. I want to have sex, too. We'll have sex. Together." It wasn't the most sterling moment in his life, but as the words came out, he didn't regret them. He wanted Tessa, he wanted to touch her, taste her, sink deep into her.

And Miss Frisky Pants, with the need to hit on every man in his building, looked him dead in the eye and said, "No."

The word was carefully enunciated, clearly spoken, with no room for misunderstanding, but Gabe was four years past no. He moved closer, skin brushing against skin. He could smell her perfume mixed with her desire, and it burned inside him.

"What's wrong, Tessa? I'm not good enough?"

She put a hand to his chest to push him back, but the touch was soft and so tempting. "Don't do this."

"Do what?"

"Don't get all stupid on me now, Gabe."

He pressed into her and her body pressed back.

"Don't come any closer," she warned.

He didn't listen. He backed her completely into the table. There was always a moment in a poker game when the bluff becomes a need, when rational logic exits the brain and all that's left is the game itself.

Her mouth was inches away. Full and waiting...

"If you kiss me, I'm going to scream," she whispered.

He took her mouth with a hunger that he had never known before. Her mouth was so soft, so perfect. And, oh, the taste of her. There was the bite of lime, the mint of toothpaste and...her. His tongue thrust into her mouth, and he felt her fingers dig into his arm.

"I'm sorry, Tessa," he said, and it was the last rational thing out of his mouth.

4

GABE. GABE. GABE.

It was Gabe who was kissing her, eating her alive, making her feel and—worst of all—making her want. Tessa wanted to kill him for it.

Tessa pushed against him—hard—because she couldn't want Gabe. Not now. She'd done that in the past, her dreams-can-come-true phase, but this time nobody—no man—would interfere. She had a plan. A career. An apartment. After that, yes. But now? No way in hell.

And especially not with Gabe.

In the world of men she trusted, there was only one, and he was currently kissing her as if he were about to have sex with her.

Gabe.

Tessa stood there, frozen, so many variations of *no* forming on her lips, but then his mouth fastened on her breast through the thin silk material and all thoughts of trust flew out the window. He sucked there, driving all doubts from her mind. Her head listed back, her knees weak because the sensations inside her were stealing the life from her.

The man swore, then pushed aside the straps of her top, and the cool night air blew across bare skin. His mouth was hard and brutal, but she didn't care. He was pulling, sucking, arousing, awakening, until her whole being shifted down to the piercing ache between her thighs.

Sweet mercy, she thought. Over and over again, Tessa focused on the pleasure, the sweet, merciful pleasure, because this was new, exquisitely new. So she closed her eyes, pretending this was some dark, handsome stranger who was making her burn. With her eyes closed, she could pretend this man wasn't Gabe.

Her hands braced against the table, because she didn't dare touch him. That much she knew. Better to stay frozen, unfeeling, than for him to guess what rash thoughts were pounding inside her brain. But then one of his hands moved lower, diving to the apex of her thighs. Tessa wanted to clamp them together, to keep her secret safe, but her body had a will of its own.

Shamelessly her thighs parted, his fingers shoving damp panties aside, and her body shook as he pushed one finger inside her.

One traitorous, decadent finger.

Oohhh…

She heard his sigh, a man finding victory.

The next few moments were a blur of skin, pleasure and erotic dreams. Her back braced against the table, and then he was there, filling her up with something much more dangerous—himself.

At first there was pain—four years was a long time—and he was big, hard and throbbing with life. Tessa didn't want to find pleasure, she wanted to keep Gabe locked in a different place, but there wasn't a choice because right now she could think of nothing but this. The smell of his body, the sharp bunch of his muscles as he moved, the sound of her sophist ideals being exterminated one spine-melting thrust at a time.

Her eyes stayed firmly shut, her fingers clenched at her side, only her muscles betraying her. Each time he drove into her, her thighs clenched tighter and tighter, automatically pulling him home.

His breathing matched hers, fast, strained, two people rapidly losing their precarious hold on sanity. For Tessa, sanity was overrated. Better to reimagine his face into a shadow. Better to cast his mouth—that talented mouth—into one that was sensual, hard and unforgiving. Her image of her dream lover settled deep in her mind, and her body shook as that fantasy man took her over and over.

Never before had it been like this, so physical, so animal, so…fascinating. He thrust hard and deep, and she whimpered.

Immediately he stopped.

"Tess?" She heard the ache in his voice, the pain, the guilt. He pulled out of her fast, but her body wasn't done. She needed this, she needed release, she needed to *come.*

"Please," she whispered.

"I'm sorry."

"Please," she tried again, her mouth dry, but she desperately needed to find that place again. It'd been so long….

"You get dressed. I'll leave you alone." He sounded so lonely, so sad, and her heart lurched. At first in pain and then in something more savage. She wasn't going to let him leave. Not until she finished. Tonight this was all about her. After four years, she had earned this one night.

"No. Must finish," she managed, low and pleading.

"Tessa?"

"Finish," she said, and this time there was a snap in her voice. A command. This was about her. About taking control. One step at a time.

Tessa waited, half expecting him to leave her decimated and desperate. Then she felt his body move, heard his breath catch, and she knew that he would cure this lonely ache inside her.

"I'll make this right," he said, picking her up in strong arms, which helped fuel the fantasy-man image. Gabe wasn't a carrier, he was a goofball without a serious bone in his body. The wide chest underneath her head? That belonged to someone else.

With those thoughts, she kept her eyes screwed shut, determined to keep his face from her mind. She heard the rustle of clothes, felt his hands gentle as he undressed her, and then his mouth was on hers—soft and seductive. She sighed a little, settling into the kiss, and strong hands stroked her, exploring and discovering her pleasures.

Denny had never been so attentive, so careful, and Tessa's mind began to soar. She was floating, high as a cloud, where the world existed only for her delight. He was hers, existing only to please her. His mouth tarried at her breast, and her back arched up, wanting to keep him close, but the merciless mouth moved lower, pressing soft, pliant kisses against her skin, her belly. Lower he moved, settling between her legs, and her heart raced because the pulse at her core was aching now, dripping with need. His lips swept the inside of her thighs, the stubble at his jaw rasping against her flesh. Wickedly he teased her, his tongue moving close, so close, so close, and she squirmed to lead his mouth where she craved.

His hands locked on her hips, and she fought to free herself, to feel him against her lips, but he continued—slow, steady, heartless. She moaned, her hands fisted against the mattress, until…

Until…

Heaven.

Slowly his tongue moved inside her, playing her at his leisure. She cried out, and his mouth turned. He captured her inner lips, sucking and pulling, hard and insistent, until she was begging, pleading because this pressure was killing her.

Frantically Tessa clawed at his shoulders, finally daring to touch him because she wanted much more than teasing. She wanted him to fill this emptiness inside her.

The dark stranger laughed, not cruelly but so knowing, and then he slid into her. Tessa sighed because this was what she needed, what her body craved. He thrust slow and deep, reaching farther and farther, as if they had all night, as if they had forever.

Still her eyes were closed, and he didn't seem to mind. Without her sight, her other senses took over, the sounds of the late-night city noise, the barges on the river, the far-off wail of a siren and the sound of breathing. Air pulling in and out. Life.

Her mouth ached to taste him, to taste the salt that she could smell on his skin. But that would be touching. That wouldn't be wise in Tessa's world. If she touched him again, she would know this man who was filling her, this man who was teaching her what pleasure could mean. And she couldn't have that because she desperately needed someone she could trust.

So she listened…and floated…and felt. Mercy, she felt. There were a thousand nerve strings inside her, stretching, pulling, threatening to break, and with each thrust the strings pulled tighter.

Tessa wanted more. "Faster," she said in a whisper. But he heard. She heard him rise over her, bringing her hips higher, and he began to move faster, pushing inside her, the strings pulling tighter and tighter.

Her body arched, taut, and she twisted with each powerful stroke because she could feel it coming closer. She could see it, the streaking lights that shone behind her lids. Harder and harder he went, this dark man she didn't want to know, touching her, taking her deeper and deeper into his world.

Higher she went….

Higher…

Higher…

And there.

Tessa came on a sigh, felt his body jerk. And then he held her close, cradling her to him. Her eyes stayed shut. Keeping his image far from her mind.

"TESSA?" GABE STUDIED HER peaceful smile, trying to figure out what part of the movie he had missed.

"Ssshhhhhh," she answered in a sleepy voice. "No names. Two strangers."

What the hell? Okay, he'd either traumatized her or screwed her into a break with reality, neither of which seemed viable.

"Tess?"

"No names," she muttered.

Nope, not that either, Gabe. "Miss?" he asked, trying to come up with some anonymous yet personal mode of address.

"What?"

"Are you okay?"

She smiled again. "I'm lovely. I feel lovely."

That didn't sound bad. "You're not hurt?"

"I think I'm going to hurt in the morning," she said, her eyes still closed, and he wished that she'd open them, look at him, so that he would know she was okay. "Can we do that again?" she asked, her voice dreamy.

"I don't know," stated Gabe, the first and only time in his life that he'd ever said no to a naked female. And Tessa was marvelously naked. Her skin was smooth, and lightly tanned, like pale scotch on a summer's night. Her breasts were firm, exactly fitting…

No, no, no…

He didn't need to be thinking about Tessa's firm breasts with nipples the color of…

Gabe shook his head.

"Let's do it again," she repeated, sending a new rush of blood to his cock.

"I can't," he lied.

"You must," she ordered, and he heard it again, that trace of Napoleon-like command in her voice. *Where the hell had that come from?*

"This is a bad idea, Te—miss," he said, but his no-conscience hard-on was ready and waiting, not really caring about personal boundaries or morning-after complications. And Gabe, at his heart, was merely a man.

"You must," she said.

Gabe, the weak-hearted coward that he was, obeyed.

THEY MADE LOVE another three times during the night because Tessa had four lost years to make up for. Four times in all, once for each year of her life that she'd given up. Her dark stranger never asked her questions again, words were rarely used at all—a fact that she was grateful for.

She wasn't going to dwell on who was next to her, wasn't going to delve into that never-never land where man dreams were supposed to come true but they instead ended up tattooed in permanent red ink. Instead she was going to focus on this pleasure, this sex, this dark stranger who could make her body ache. As long as she didn't think about who he was, her heart—and her own Tessa dreams—were safe.

Finally, when the morning sun was creeping through the window, she fell asleep, curled up next to him, feeling the dusting of chest hair tickling her back, feeling his flaccid sex settling comfortably between her thighs, feeling his lips soft against her neck.

Tessa smiled and fell into a sated, dreamless sleep.

THE PHONE RANG, hellishly loud, and Gabe reached out a hand, searching for it.

"Did you see her naked yet?"

Instantly Gabe was wide-awake. The word *naked* did that to a guilty man.

"What?" he asked, focusing on Sean's voice, keeping his attentions far away from the trim, tight body that was currently curled into his Johnson as if she owned it. Which she did.

Gabe sprang out of bed.

"Did you see her naked yet?" Sean repeated. "Daniel put money on one night, but I knew you were too honorable to do anything more than sneak a long look when she came out of the shower. So? Listen, bro, I could use the inside track on this one. The Mets' losing streak is killing my discretionary income, and I was counting on something to bail me out. Any fever looks last night?"

"What's a fever look?" asked Gabe, already knowing the answer.

"I know you don't get 'em like I do, but it's the sloe-eyed thing that women do when they want to test out your equipment. So...Tessa giving you the sloe-eyes?"

Gabe turned his back to the bed, not wanting to know if Tessa was giving him the sloe-eyes, at least not while he was on the phone with his brother. "Nothing. I went to a party last night. Fell asleep. Get your mind out of the gutter." He heard a soft moan, and his mind, still in the gutter, turned to see the naked female in his bed.

The tight, trim body stirred under the covers, a tousled head of honey-brown hair starting to emerge. Gabe pushed her head back down before she forgot she was wearing no clothes.

"Sucks," answered Sean, master of the crude yet precisely effective come-back. "Better luck next—"

"What do you want?" interrupted Gabe, searching for his shorts and finding them hung over the lamp. While pulling them on, he kept one eye glued to the dark head, waiting for signs of life—or anger, whichever came first.

"I wanted to talk to you about the building permit for the renovations...."

One green eye opened, widened in horror, nothing even close to sloe-eyed fever.

"'Bye, Sean. We'll talk later," Gabe finished, quickly slamming down the phone.

Tessa bolted upright, clutching the blanket like a lifeline.

"Tessa?" he asked carefully, fully prepared for a five-alarm tongue-lashing on the proper respect for personal boundaries.

Gradually the alarm in her eyes dimmed.

"I'm fine," she answered, dodging his gaze.

Gabe heaved a glorious sigh of relief and began pulling on his jeans. He had screwed up royally last night, he knew it, but this moment of forgiveness—nay, acceptance—really did his heart good. "I can bunk with Daniel if you want—if it'll make you feel better."

It was a generous, unselfish offer, designed to give her some level of comfort and security. An assurance that as tempting as her bones were, Gabe had the necessary self-control to modify his behavior and not jump them—again.

She licked her lips, a nervous gesture, which really shouldn't have turned him on, but did anyway.

"I'm not kicking you out of your own apartment," she answered, immediately sensing the nobleness of his offer. "There's lots of room here."

Gabe stroked his chin, then realized he needed to shave. But first it was time for The Talk. Reestablish the ground rules she so desperately needed. Who would have guessed that little Tessa could be such a demon princess in bed? Gabe shook off the momentary lapse. "Tessa, we're friends—"

Quickly she interrupted, obviously sensing where the conversation was headed. "Don't worry about that. Can you turn around?" she asked primly.

Gabe nodded, obediently turning the other way. Not that she realized that the window reflection provided a crystal-clear vision of tawny flesh.

Gabe wisely opted not to tell her.

AFTER GABE LEFT TO set up the bar, Tessa showered, dressed, and then sat cross-legged on the floor contemplating the ramifications of last nights encounter with the dark stranger, which she categorized under "Erotic Fantasy" rather than "Sex With a Man that She Really Needed to Trust Because So Few Men Understood Her Desire for Independence After Denny Had Upended Her Life, and Gabe Was One of the Only Ones Who Treated Her Well."

Before she let herself go gaga over the dark stranger, her first priority was moving out—*muy pronto*. One thing about sunlight: it shined a glaring laser beam on all the weaknesses that she was currently experiencing in her life. The D on her accounting test. Denny-gate—the scandalous turnabout on all his previously sacred vows of never wanting family and a life with a ball and chain. The apartment in Hudson Towers, just waiting for the occupancy of a mature, independent woman who could survive New York on her own. Most thrilling, the purple hickey on her stomach, which looked so much more decadent than the letters D-E-N-N-Y on her butt. And lastly but not leastly, the well-used ache between her legs.

Who knew the dark stranger was so…knowing in the mysteries of female sexuality? Tessa grinned. It was an experience well worth repeating. However, now wasn't the time to drift from her life purpose. She pulled out her laptop and scoured the online listings for roommates wanted. When she found anything remotely suitable, she dashed off a response, before finally posting an ad of her own.

Eventually the calling of the listings took over, and Tessa did what she always did when she needed to escape: she browsed through the apartment rentals section, seeing what was what, all the while lamenting the high rents. So, a girl could dream. However, dreams were meaningless without the financial capital to achieve them, so she pulled out her accounting book and tried to study. For three hours she sat there, studying, but none of the concepts seemed to hold her attention.

The principles of accrued depreciation were losing out to the principles of last night. She could still feel his hands on her skin, hear the rush of his breath and smell the musky desire in the air. And the way he touched her down below... wow. Pretty soon her body was flushed all over again.

The book sat in front of her, the page on depreciation unturned, and the beginnings of a plan formed in her mind. Maybe there was a way to have it all. If she moved out, put the necessary distance between them, then maybe she could have her independence and her mystery lover, too. A nighttime diversion in the shadows to experience more of that expanding-of-her-life stuff, with none of the glaring laser beams of daylight to worry about. It just might work. Her decision made, she went back to studying because, yes, she had a real career to prepare for.

When her watch said five, she knew it was time to go earn a living, so she tugged on her T-shirt and jeans and took the subway in to work.

Tuesday nights were traditionally slow, a mix of old-time regulars and the spring-fever crowds who showed up early and clocked out early, as well.

Gabe was behind the bar, pulling a beer for Charlie, who had worked as a union boss since before the Eisenhower administration. Next to Charlie was Lloyd, who had worked as an ironworker for nearly sixty years before retiring five years ago. Next to Lloyd was EC, a tall stick of a man who had worked as an engineer for MTA for sixty years in order to keep his two ex-wives in blue fox furs. And finally there was Syd, a retired police detective who, at fifty-one, was the young one in the bunch. They all had been coming to Prime for longer than Tessa had worked there, longer than even Gabe.

Gabe.

He shouldn't look any different from yesterday, because men don't suddenly morph overnight, but everything about him was sharper, bigger, harder, possibly because she remembered in minute detail exactly what he felt like when he was on top of her.

Determined to act as if she wasn't puddling giddiness on the inside, Tessa smoothed out her perpetually wrinkled T-shirt. Then casually she smiled and waved at them all, and Charlie patted the empty bar stool next to him.

"Tessa, come around and keep an old man company for a while. You know this ticker is going to give out any minute, and I want to die happy with a beautiful woman at my side."

Tessa was used to Charlie's banter and settled next to him. "Your eyesight is going bad, Charlie. Nobody's called me beautiful since—actually, never."

"We take a vote," he announced. "Democracy in action. All who think Tessa is beautiful raise your hand."

"Will it get me a whiskey on the house?" asked Lloyd, but he raised his hand anyway. Three other hands rose, and EC glared at Gabe, who eventually raised his hand, too, carefully not looking in Tessa's direction and—jeez, was he blushing?

Lloyd laughed, a loud burst of noise that was half joy and half bronchitis. "See there. Never argue with a man who wants to pay you a compliment."

"Well, thank you then. I think you're only warming up for tonight. Who's the lucky lady, gents?"

Charlie coughed, pushing at creaky silver spectacles. "There is one."

Tessa looked at him because it was easier to flirt with the regulars than to do casual conversation with Gabe. She could feel his eyes on her, careful, watching, and she didn't dare look at him. Charlie was the perfect diversion. She balanced her chin on her palm. "Tell me all about it."

He took a long drink of beer, gathering his courage before speaking. "There was a woman in here Tuesday last. Sure enough, she looked familiar to me, but when you're pushing eighty, a man has a lot of women in his past. She was my age and walked like the queen, but I felt this stirring, an old song playing in my head. She came in with what must have been her granddaughter. Young blonde with wide blue eyes. Either one of you remember their names? Driving me crazy trying to recall. Damned Alzheimer's.

"Carrie tells me I'm starting to lose my memory, but I keep denying it. I mean, how many seniors do you know that can remember the last home game of the Brooklyn Dodgers or MacArthur's ticker-tape parade in '51? That was when New York meant something. That was history. Like the days when Paddy O'Sullivan refused to sell a whiskey to Spiro T. because Paddy didn't like his politics." Charlie sighed, lifting his beer to his mouth. "Those were the days."

Gabe smiled, shook his head. "Sorry, Charlie. Wish I could help you out."

"Well, buy me another beer to help me forget your transgression. Maybe they'll come in tonight. I wore my best tie." He looked down at the open-collar shirt. "Oops. Guess I forgot that, too."

Tessa laughed. "You look mighty handsome, Charlie. Was the girl in a yellow sundress?"

Charlie snapped his fingers. "There you go! Remember her name?"

Tessa gave him an easy grin. "No, but I really liked the dress." She looked up at the clock, casually dodging Gabe's eye. "Gotta start busting my butt, Charlie. Boss is a real nutjob about punching the clock."

Then Tessa shot said boss a sweet smile and went about her job as if nothing had ever happened at all.

5

GABE CHATTED WITH THE codgers who had been regulars when Uncle Patrick was alive and would probably be regulars until they died. Considering how much Gabe had learned about old New York, he hoped that wasn't anytime soon, because he had yet to hear the long-promised story about the night EC saw the Blue Shirts lose to the Canadiens in Madison Square Garden in, as EC so poignantly described it, "the heartbreaker of the century."

However, tonight he kept a careful eye on Tessa, making sure that the status quo had been restored. Everything seemed right, but as the night wore on, he found himself less concerned with the status quo and more concerned with the eye-candy job of watching her.

At first it was big, general things that he'd overlooked about her before. Her long fingers twisting the cap off a beer in one graceful slide. The way her body moved so easily in soft, faded jeans. The sound of her laugh when Lloyd tossed out a bad joke. Over time, his focus narrowed and the smaller details began to emerge. The way she curled her lower lip in when she was shaking a martini, the way she brushed the hair from her face, the way her green eyes worked the customers, always friendly, capable, always the best friend behind the bar.

One thing about Tessa—she was an original. And people knew it when they talked to her. She never said much about herself, only listening. Always listening.

At half past seven a college baseball team pounded in fresh from a hard-won victory—judging by the dirt-stained jerseys. Tessa didn't blink an eye. Instead she filled twenty-seven orders, including nine Long Island Iced Teas. As she worked, she twirled the glasses in the air, flirted with them all, easy and friendly, but they sucked it up like flies to honey. Gabe shook his head in amazement, still watching, though, if only to make sure everybody stayed in line.

Underneath the shell there was something fragile. Last night Gabe had broken something inside her and he wasn't sure what. That sort of responsibility didn't sit well with an Irish Catholic who prided himself on doing the right thing.

The time flew until it was nearly nine and Daniel came in to prepare the night deposit. Daniel was the antithesis of Sean, quiet, reserved and always alone. Although only four years older than Gabe, Daniel had lived through nightmares that Gabe could never imagine.

Daniel had been married for only five months when his new wife had been killed in the North Tower. She and Daniel both worked for an accounting firm there, and Daniel had been getting coffee for her from the Starbucks that was a few blocks north. He had been running late. Michelle had been at work precisely on time.

The aftershocks of 9/11 had been hard on the family—their mother had been alive then—but Daniel never fell apart. His whole life he had never said much, but he did change. Now he watched the world with grave eyes, never missing the details. While Gabe could joke with Sean, Gabe was always nervous about Daniel, never knowing exactly what to say or not to say. It was a bad feeling for a bartender. It was hell for a brother.

"No winner on the pool?" he asked Gabe, his gaze resting on Tessa. Gabe drew in a tense breath because he'd been hoping to avoid the subject of the bet. Actually, he was hoping that everyone would forget about it, but with such a large pot that seemed doubtful.

"What pool?" asked Lloyd.

"Never mind," said Tessa quickly, a little too quickly— noticed Gabe, not daring to look in her direction.

Daniel looked at Gabe, looked at Tessa, eyes assessing, then he shrugged. "Did Sean call you this morning?"

In that moment Gabe knew he'd drawn a reprieve. "Yeah, but he hung up before he told me anything."

"Somebody's been asking questions about your license."

"What license?"

"Liquor."

Gabe swore. "I thought computers were supposed to make our lives better. Instead people don't take responsibility for shit and the screwups get shuffled from one department to another."

Daniel cut him off. "Don't worry. Sean said he knew a girl in the planning department who had a sister who works in beverage control. He'll get it squared away, but it might hold up the building permit for the place next door for a few weeks."

"I really can't afford to sit on empty real estate for a few weeks, you know? Why does everything take so freaking long?"

"What's with you?"

"Patience is overrated, Daniel."

Lloyd laughed, then coughed and then lifted his glass. "But a good man's credit isn't. Can you pour me another scotch and water, Gabe?"

IT WAS TWENTY MINUTES after closing and the bar was empty. The regulars had left with a chorus of goodbyes, and Daniel had carted off a night deposit that would help offset the cost of the renovations for the space next door. Assuming there was going to be a space next door.

Tessa poured the leftover ice into the sink and began scrubbing down the stainless-steel countertop. She worked quietly, leaving him alone, but he could hear her thinking. Normally the problem with the building permit was something he'd confide in her, but normal didn't feel right anymore. Sex could do that to two people.

Finally, she laid down her rag. "Is something wrong?"

"Nothing," snapped Gabe. She stared, silently calling him a liar, and he sighed. "Nothing I can't handle."

"You're ready to get started next door, aren't you?"

Yeah, he was more than ready. As soon as he'd seen the place go up for sale, he'd swooped in for the buy, killing his finances in the process, but it'd be worth it. When Gabe committed, he was in it for the long haul, and the restoration would be perfect. "I can start on some of it myself. Nobody will know."

"You should get Daniel to help," said Tessa.

"He's got enough to think about without having to share in my responsibilities, as well."

"He's part owner."

"'The silent part' is what he always says."

"I can help," she offered. "Dad was pretty handy around the house, and I've been known to perform electrical work for food."

Here was Tessa, no place to live, struggling to find a real career, and she wanted to help. "Thanks, but don't worry about it."

Quietly Tessa went back to work, and Gabe closed off the taps. Another few minutes passed before she spoke again.

"You didn't say anything to Daniel, did you? One day. He called it. He should have won the pool."

Yes, Daniel should have won the pool. Yes, the world should know what a weakhearted bastard Gabe was, but Gabe wasn't ready to admit that yet. "Do you really want me to say something, Tessa? Let the pool go. In a few days everybody will forget about it, they'll be betting on horse races, and then I'll get Sean to refund the money."

"I don't like being dishonest." She pulled a hand through her hair, her breasts lifting with the movement. Gabe didn't want to notice, but he did.

"It's better if everybody knows?"

She met his eyes, and Gabe felt a stirring in his gut, a stirring of blood that would only mean trouble, especially for her. "Did you hate last night?" she asked.

Here it was, nearly one in the morning, and Tessa wanted to talk. Now.

Outside, the late-night streets were quiet and still. Inside, Gabe felt as though there were an impending nuclear explosion. Okay, fine, she wanted to talk? He would talk. "It's biologically impossible for a man to hate or regret sex. Everything else is within the realm of possibility. But sex? No."

"Oh," she said and went back to wiping the counter, which even a moron could see was already spotless.

So the time for talking was now over. Gabe should feel happy. She could work. He could work, so he scanned over the inventory behind the three bars, counting stock for the next day, but the numbers started running together in his head.

Finally he stopped counting. "What does 'oh' mean?"

"Just 'oh.'"

She sounded miffed, slightly defensive and hurt. The miffed he could handle, the defensive was completely normal, but the hurt was like a hot poker against his heart. So the time for talking was *not* over. "Tessa?"

She put down her rag. "I liked it," she said, which came out like a confession rather than a compliment.

Gabe chose to ignore that important point and smiled. "I know."

"At least once I got to the part where I could separate you from the other man."

Gabe blinked. "What other man?"

She worked her mouth, struggling to explain, but eventually she got there. "You know, the not-you other man. Anyway, once I got over that hump, figuratively speaking, it was great. I didn't know it could be like that."

This time she gave him a half smile. Almost shy. And right then, it didn't matter if it was one in the morning and he'd had three hours of sleep. Right at the moment Gabe could have scaled the George Washington Bridge single-handedly.

"Gabe?"

"What?" he asked, starting to like this conversation. Gabe wasn't nearly the horndog that Sean was. Gabe worked too hard and didn't worry a lot about sex. There was usually a willing female when his body got too tense. Yet this time it was Tessa and things were different. Last night had been different. He'd wanted to please her, wanted to make her scream.

Gabe had never thought about lust that way, never felt the hard kick inside him. But last night some switch had flipped on inside him, and now that he had gotten used to the sudden atomic surges in his cock, gotten used to the low-grade hum in his brain, he wasn't ready to flip the switch back off again.

Weakling.

"Could we keep pretending?" Tessa asked.

"Pretending what?" he asked, wondering what pretending had to do with sex.

She waved a hand, searching for words. "Pretending that you're…somebody else. For instance, a mysterious stranger who I don't know and who never tells me his name."

Ah, the male ego. Such a powerful force, so easily annihilated. Gabe looked at her, wondering what strategic move he'd done wrong last night, because it was obvious that while he'd been thinking *screaming,* she'd been thinking *somebody else.*

"I'm not sure I like that game." Which was more polite than *Hell, no.*

"You liked it fine last night," she reminded him.

"I didn't know that's the game we were playing last night. Hell, Tessa, I didn't even know we were playing a game. I don't know. I don't think you're ready. It's only been four years—" *Jeez* "—you need to ease back into things. You shouldn't have to pretend," he said. *Especially with me*, he thought, keeping quiet on that one.

Her cheeks were flushed, not with anger but embarrassment, and Gabe couldn't figure out why this game thing was so important to her, but he was willing to try and understand. For Tessa, he would trudge onward to comprehend the great unknown that was the female brain.

"It's difficult for me because we're friends, and I don't want to mess with that, but I liked last night. I really liked last night and I think if I thought of you as someone else other than you—my friend—then it'd be easier. Does that make sense?"

Gabe considered it. "No."

She frowned in frustration and then tried again. "A healthy fantasy life should be part of every woman's innate sexuality," she told him, sounding like something on a TV talk show. Maybe that's where this was coming from? Maybe Tessa had decided to start living again and she thought Gabe was safe.

That should have been a comforting thought.

Gabe was uncomforted.

He leaned one hip against the bar, not sure what to say.

Tessa reached out a hand, touched him on the arm. One touch that felt like a brand. "Please."

"You're sure about this?"

Tessa shot him a cocky smile, the one she always used right before torching her Flaming Lemon Drop shooter. "Oh, yeah."

She sounded so confident, so capable, so…turned on. Maybe he'd misjudged last night. Maybe there was no reason for all his guilt. And then her body shifted, drawing his eyes. The scent of her, of Tessa, filled his mind until he couldn't think. His blood heated, and right then Gabe really didn't care about cleaning up or closing down. He needed to kiss that cocky mouth. Needed to touch her again.

He pulled her close and molded her to him, feeling the vulnerability, feeling the rightness of it. He looked down at her face, the eyes so carefully closed, but he didn't worry about that. He needed to take that mouth again.

And it was exactly like last night. That same blaze ignited inside him. Her mouth was soft, so teasingly soft, and it opened easily for him, as if it was his own private stock. His hands traced over her, finding the places that he already knew. Gabe's body, his cock, his hands, his mouth, already knew the game—and couldn't wait.

Tonight she wrapped her arms around him, touching him in ways that she hadn't last night. Her hand reached down, cupped him through his jeans, and he nearly shot off right there.

He wasn't like this, he kept reminding himself. He didn't lose it like Sean. But, damn, he was inches away from losing it now. He wanted to take her there, in the bar, with the lights shining from overhead, and he knew he needed to get control.

Her uncontrollable hand reached for the button at his fly, and he stopped worrying about the damned protocol. Desperately Gabe fumbled for the light switch, sighing with relief when darkness fell, only the dim glow of the city shining in from the front windows.

No one would know. No one would know but Tessa and Gabe.

He stopped her hand before she got farther because he was close to bursting—and they hadn't even started. Not yet.

Purposefully Gabe grabbed her hand, walked her around the bar and then sat her up on the bar stool. Not satisfied with the situation, he eased off her shirt and bra, finding the soft skin that he was rapidly developing a taste for. Now the situation was looking up.

Tonight Tessa was bolder with him, running her hands under his shirt, removing the soft cotton, leaving them skin to skin. He wrapped her jean-clad legs around his waist, his body seeking home, eager to find the moist honey that Gabe knew was waiting there.

Tessa grinded against him with painful friction, and his body jerked, impatient with the layers between them.

One way to fix that. He wrenched down her zipper, his hands already reaching beneath the tight material, underneath the damp fabric, finding the warm pulsing piece of her that he wanted to own.

Tessa moaned in his mouth, and he hauled her off the stool, stripping her jeans in one easy pull. The lean legs wrapped around him, and he set his erection free. With shaking fingers, he sheathed himself and then slammed into her core.

He swallowed her cry with his kiss, tasting the tang of lemon, the softness that was Tessa. And because she liked to prove him wrong, her hips surged against him, and the firelust began all over again.

Five times he moved inside her, but the angle was wrong. Not enough. Not deep enough. Not enough of her. Frustrated, he swore and lifted her onto the bar, following on top of her. This time when he drove into her, he heard her answering sounds, music to his mind.

Suddenly, strong legs wound tightly around his waist. That was what he loved most about being inside her, this urgent desire to have him closer and closer until their bodies fit together like one.

Her hand fisted against his back, and he could feel the hunger that was raging inside her.

"I like the dark," she whispered, her lips tasting his neck. "I love the dark."

"Tessa," he said but then stopped. Gabe wasn't used to talking, wasn't used to the games that women and men played.

He'd always been obsessed with Prime, but this…a man could develop a new obsession.

"No names," she whispered and then twisted in a neat little turn, climbing on top.

The dim light hit her body, her skin shimmering in the shadows, her breasts glistening with moisture, and his heart all but stopped. Her head fell to one side, her neck so long, so smooth, and his heart started beating again, hammering against his chest. He felt it then, desire, fear and the absolute certainty that he had crossed over some imaginary line, a point where there was no going back. Ever.

Tessa rode him, bucked against him, her hands skimming over his skin, and Gabe knew he was close. He grabbed her hips tight, plunged inside her, pistoning back and forth, wanting to pull her over the edge, wanting to watch her face as she came. Soon her mouth fell slack, her body tensed and, with a long cry, she climaxed, pulling him in after her.

IN THE DARKNESS, SO many things could stay hidden. Tessa felt his body beneath hers, marveled at the strength there, imagined the long hours that had made him that way.

He was her pool boy, her landscaper, her repairman and her delivery man, all wrapped up into one neat package of her ideal lover. That knowledge she could accept, letting the fantasy weave over her, keeping her mind free to explore, to enjoy and, best of all, to savor. As long as he was nothing more than a fantasy, she could look at him with a lover's eyes. Tessa could still make love to him, and all she had to do was pretend. Not a problem.

She rose and dressed, watching the play of the muscles in his chest, his butt as he put on his clothes. The lines of his body were so hard and fluid, like a sculpture but alive and burning with heat.

"Tessa," he started and then stopped, and she was grateful that he understood, that he never questioned why their relationship must stay in the dark. But there were so many places to go, so many other places that lovers could meet in secret.

"I think we should meet at a movie next time," she told him, daring to propose something new. "In the afternoon, when nobody's there, in the back row."

"I don't know," he muttered, his voice unsure. "Are you still playing the game?"

She laid a finger on his lips, pressed a kiss against his chest. "Ssshhh. Think. Fantasize. So many things to do in the dark. Tomorrow. Meet me tomorrow afternoon."

Her heart raced, pumping with excitement at the idea of seeing her lover again so soon. He reached for her, kissed her with passion, eagerness, devotion, and soon she could feel the decision inside him.

"All right."

WHEN GABE FLIPPED ON the bar lights, he expected to find Tessa still caught up in the last throes of passion. Instead she was unaffected, her face smiling, with none of the husky thrill that he'd heard in her voice earlier.

Inside, Gabe knew perfectly well that something was screwed, but his body still hummed from being surrounded by her, and for the moment he could convince himself that everything was fine.

They closed up together, Tessa whistling a Donna Summer song as she finished, and then he walked with her to the subway, back to the apartment they both shared. Once inside, he looked at her curiously, wanting to hold her again but not daring to ask.

She gave him a careless smile and waved before shutting her bedroom door. "See you in the morning."

Gabe contemplated the closed door, contemplated his aching cock and decided on a shower.

Cold.

THE CHIRPING SOUND OF Tessa's cell woke Gabe bright and early on Wednesday morning. He didn't intend to eavesdrop on his roommate's conversation, but she certainly wasn't making an effort to hide her words, talking loudly, and then his ears perked up at four of them *two-bedroom, one-bath*.

The more he listened, the guiltier he felt, but not so guilty that he would stop. She made noises of general agreement, tossed out some numbers and in general seemed happy as a clam.

Gabe frowned.

When she wandered into the living room, he was already waiting for her. "Phone call?" he asked.

"Yeah," she replied, a stupid answer that didn't help him at all.

"Oh. Making plans for tonight?" he asked, trying again. "Remember, you're supposed to work. It's my poker night."

"No plans," she said breezily.

"What was it then?" he asked, which sounded so pathetically obvious, but, okay, lately he seemed to be losing his usual subtle touch.

"My potential new roommate," she replied, beaming at him.

Roommate? What the hell? Now, sure, they were only on day two of the Great Roommate Experiment, but in Gabe's world, things were good. "A new roommate? What the heck is that about?"

"I told you that I'd be out of your hair as soon as I could."

Yes, that had been the plan before they were sleeping together. "That's really fast. What do you know about this person?"

"Well, Dad, funny you should ask, but I think you'd approve. He owns a bakery in the East Village, has a dog named Butch and is subleasing a fab two-bed, one-bath convertible in Hamilton Heights. It's no Hudson Towers, is slightly more modern than I like, but on the plus side, there's lot of square footage, the rent is good and he sounds reasonable."

"A guy?" he repeated stupidly.

Tessa folded her arms across her chest. "Since I'm currently living with a male, I decided I should expand my horizons."

"I thought you weren't going to live with a guy."

"Do you have a penis, Gabe?"

Gabe let that remark slide. "He's a stranger."

"You were my friend," she said, possibly a jab below the belt but the truth nonetheless.

"That's low, Tessa. I'm still your friend," he told her, letting the truth wash off his back like a duck. Sleeping with someone and being friends with them were not mutually exclusive. *Except with Tessa,* a little voice reminded him. Gabe told the little voice to shut up.

"I can't live with someone who doesn't respect my personal boundaries," she answered. "I can't live with someone without having boundaries, and if we're having sex, the boundaries don't work."

Now she wanted to talk about personal boundaries? He had thought they'd gotten past that about the sixth time he'd seen her naked. And now she was contemplating moving in with a complete stranger who, for all she knew could be a serial killer? Something was totally wrong in this picture, and he kept his temper, choosing his words carefully but still pissed. "I respect your personal boundaries. For God's sake, I'm the only freaking person who's going to respect your personal boundaries. Did you notice who left your toothbrush untouched on the sink this morning? That was me. And did you see who saved the last bit of milk for you even though I can't drink my coffee without it? Me again."

"I didn't know I was an inconvenience," she mumbled, and there was something in her green eyes. Pain. He recognized it. And, yes, he was a jerk.

Gawd.

Gabe collapsed into his favorite chair, wondering why it seemed as if they were suddenly speaking in different languages. Was sex really such a friendship killer? *This is Tessa*, the little voice reminded him. Gabe tried again. "I don't want you to think you have to move out. It's not bad with you here, honestly. Actually, it's nice having someone else around." It was the truth.

The pain faded from her eyes—thankfully. But Tessa still didn't look convinced.

"This is temporary, Gabe. We always said it was temporary. Don't try changing things on me. I don't like change that I don't initiate, I don't handle it well and in general it freaks me out. I don't like being freaked out. Let me look at the apartment. I may hate it," she added, which he knew was supposed to make him feel better.

"Okay," he agreed, still not feeling better.

"I'll see you at the movie," she added, and he stared after her, trying to comprehend all that was her but not. The movie was probably a bad idea, but nothing in the world could keep him away.

THE THEATER WAS DARK when she arrived. She'd worn a skirt, new high heels, and wickedly enough, no panties. She found him waiting for her in the last row. They'd picked a deathly dull foreign movie six weeks into its run, so the place was empty except for Tessa.

And Xavier.

Last night she had started to think of him as Xavier when she'd lain alone in bed and remembered their stolen moments together. She couldn't call him by his real name, so she'd picked another name. A name so far from who he was that she never worried about confusing the two.

Tessa picked a seat that was one down from him, wanting to feel as if they were strangers. It was more fun if they were strangers.

Today he wore a baseball cap which hid his face from her,

everything except for the full curve of his mouth, which she would recognize across a crowded room, across a packed stadium and most thrillingly, when it touched her lips.

She smiled at the floor, adjusting her skirt across her knees, not wanting to act too forward, but she wasn't used to this, wasn't used to casual affairs hidden in secret.

His fingers rested on the armrest, inching toward her bare legs, her skirt, yet she was an inch out of his reach. She saw his frown and smiled. He slid down one seat, the cushions so close she could smell him, feel him, his arm hot against her own.

When the lights dimmed, the commercials played, meaningless words, because she was only aware of him. His fingers drifted closer, so close that if she moved only one small centimeter, they would be touching. Music blared through the speakers, causing her to jump, and in that moment his hand captured her thigh, hot and purposeful. She longed to clamp her legs together, but then he would know her weakness. Still, it wasn't long before the fingers moved. Sliding innocently back and forth along the bare skin of her thigh.

The air was chilled, and she liked his comforting touch, but then the cunning fingers moved beneath her skirt, sliding closer to her heat. This time she did clamp her thighs closed. She heard his laugh, soft, and the fingers returned, gently pleading, seeking entrance to the secret place she denied him.

Tessa hesitated, unsure, but the fingers were so warm, so comforting, and so finally she slid her thighs apart, only a bit. But it was enough.

Xavier found her warmth easily, stroking her, making her squirm in her seat. Each time he moved across her lips, her muscles gripped him here, and she slid down in her seat, wanting to feel more of this wickedness. He laughed again, took his finger in his mouth and licked.

Tessa groaned and he laughed again. Low, because he knew what this was doing to her. This time he took her in his lap, and she could feel his hardness against her rear. While she sat, the movie began to play—and so did Xavier.

Now, without any barrier to her, he stroked her at his leisure, his fingers pushing inside her, playing with her tortured flesh.

Tessa squirmed again, feeling naked and exposed, but he didn't release her. Instead his arms surrounded her, his erection pushing against her, harder, firmer, and she liked that part. Liked that she could control him, as well.

She slid her thighs farther apart to give him free rein and to more brazenly slide against him. She did, twice, feeling his thickness prod beneath her, before his arms stilled her. She fidgeted in his lap, expressing her displeasure, and felt his answering jerk of flesh. This time it was she who laughed.

"You like that?" he asked, his lips against her ear. Then he whispered more words, his fingers curling inside her, using his hands to make good on his urgent promises.

Tessa felt a sudden moan rise up inside her, forgetting the game for a moment. She wanted more; her whole body shook with it. She wanted more than his hands and she reached down between them, grasping him in a crude gesture that communicated much more than words.

He didn't need her to ask twice. She felt his hand working his pants and heard the crinkle of a foil wrapper. She sat there, waiting, waiting, waiting, until silently, easily, he repositioned her on his lap, sliding deep inside.

This time Tessa did moan, louder than she'd intended, because this was sweet relief, filling her up. Slowly he lifted her, then she slid back down on his slick flesh, slick because of her. It was an odd feeling of being empty, then slowly possessed by someone else, his body so deeply embedded inside her.

Her head fell back against his shoulder, and he kissed her neck. Such a small, simple kiss, not the passionate kiss of her fantasy lover but the kiss of someone else, a kiss that would jolt a woman right out of her fantasy. Tessa half rose in his lap, the fantasy over, and he didn't understand. He thought she was still playing the game.

He held her tight against the chair back in front of them, entering her from behind, and she knew who was there. She could feel the tightness in her chest, she could feel him, taste him, smell him.

This is Gabe.

Again and again he pushed inside her, bearing down on all the barriers that she had built up around her. He filled her so completely, so totally, and she couldn't fight this. Her body couldn't fight it. Even more dangerously, her mind couldn't fight it either. Pleasure, exquisite pleasure, overwhelmed her, pleasure so exquisite that it hurt, white-hot and splitting her in two. Again and again he moved, and she wanted to scream. In satisfaction and in fury. But Tessa couldn't. She'd kept the sound inside her for too long. Finally she came, soundlessly.

A long, long moment passed and she could feel him still inside her, feel his arms around her, and she knew. It would be so easy with Gabe. So easy to believe that with him she didn't need to worry about a thing in her life. No apartment, no career. Just one man and a woman, alone.

Then he pulled out of her, his arms disappeared, and Tessa hurriedly tidied her skirt, her fingers silently skimming over the tatooed letters on her backside.

There were things to do, an apartment to find, a career to prepare for.

Quickly Tessa left before she did something stupid for the second time in her life.

6

FORTY MINUTES LATER, Tessa had changed into blue jeans and a ragged T-shirt and then went to talk to a man about an apartment. The Hamilton Heights building had been built in the seventies, and had central AC, but the place itself had no character, no soul. Samuel was a nice enough man, with a well-trained English bulldog, and he needed a renter now, but he wasn't roommate material. Not really.

Pathetically enough, her standards had changed. Sex with Gabe had done that to her. Weakened her.

Tessa told Samuel that she was allergic to dogs and left him and his bulldog, wishing them both good luck.

Her next stop was crosstown to West End Avenue. Hudson Towers.

Tessa needed the visual reminder, the tangible piece of real estate that represented what she *knew* she was capable of achieving. At eighteen, she'd been so full of dreams before she'd met Denny, and then Denny became her life and her dream—but man dreams weren't going to pay her rent. No way would she let Gabe become Denny redux.

Get a life, she told herself and then promptly remembered she was working to get a life, which was why she was standing her at the exterior of Hudson Towers instead of going to Accounting class. Tessa might have poor decision-making skills, but at least she was self-aware enough to know it.

On that note, she grabbed a coffee and sat inside a bus

shelter, watching the tenants as they entered and left the building. Power suits and biking shorts. Smart sundresses and yoga pants. These were people who knew what they wanted in life and how to get it.

Tessa took in her own crummy T-shirt and wondered what key piece was missing from her DNA. Recently she'd been sidetracked from her goals, but all she needed to do was regain her focus. Regain her independence. Maybe she wasn't as tough as her brother, but deep inside she was a Hart and she could do this. She knew she could.

For some time she sat there, staring, visualizing, sucking in life and letting the neighborhood genes seep into her spirit. This was her dream, and nobody—*nobody*—was going to distract her from it. Eventually she rose from the bench, a new resolve firmly in place, and headed off for work.

Tonight it was she and Lindy behind the bar, which was always fun. Tessa liked Lindy, who knew more dirty jokes than most Vegas comedians and always smiled no matter the tip. Lindy had come from Trenton, but had a Malibu tan and short, bleached-blond hair to match. Plus, she was multi-talented, able to not only waitress but bartend, as well.

"Busy?" asked Tessa, automatically reaching underneath the counter to start refilling the stock of bar napkins and coasters.

"Slow as Peter's salami-hiding skills—and just as rewarding."

Tessa was never sure if Peter was real, or only a figment of Lindy's imagination, not that it really mattered. Lindy's stories were always full of "Peter this" and "Peter that."

"You need to get yourself a real man," answered Tessa.

Lindy smiled. "I have a real man. I call him my vibrator."

Tessa laughed, checking the inventory against the par sheet and counting her till. As always, things balanced exactly. As the Wednesday night happy-hour crowd began to appear, Tessa got busy pouring drinks, telling jokes and listening to the trials and tribulations of a world that simply needed a drink.

A woman in a suit came up to Tessa, ordered a low-carb wheatgrass martini and waited for the drink, eyeing the pictures on the wall behind the bar. The customer's focus was caught on one particular picture, and Tessa, idly playing the "who's she eyeballing?" game, accidentally upended the martini glass, drenching the woman in vodka.

"Oh, God!" Tessa exclaimed, reaching for a towel. It'd been over three years since she'd spilled a drink on a customer. Tessa was getting clumsy—a bartender's curse.

Thankfully there was a good-natured smile on the woman's perfectly lipsticked mouth. "Don't worry about it. I needed to get the suit dry-cleaned anyway."

"It's a great suit," Tessa said honestly. "I'll take care of the dry cleaning."

"Get over it. I am."

And immediately Tessa liked her. The woman introduced herself as Marisa Beckworth, who had had a bad day and had come in for a quick pick-me-up after work.

"Where do you work?"

"Cocoran."

Tessa put down the shaker. "You guys are the best," Tessa stated, trying not to gush but failing.

"You're not in real estate, are you?" asked Marisa, being impressively polite considering that Tessa had just drenched her.

"No, I'm studying to be an accountant."

"Oh."

"But I am looking for an apartment right now."

"I could help you out," offered Marisa, smoothly pulling out her card.

"To be honest, I know where I want to live, only I have to figure out how to get in there."

"The Dakota?"

Tessa laughed. "Do I look delusional? No, Hudson Towers, on West End."

Marisa nodded. "That's a great building, but the waiting list is a mile long and the rumor is that it's headed for co-op."

There was always something. "The thing is, it's not like I want to live there forever. I just want to live by myself for a while, and my choices in this city are currently limited to Hudson Towers and, yes, Hudson Towers."

"Manhattan. I understand completely. Do you ever watch the obituaries?"

"Not like I should."

"Who has the time, right? I bet you spend all your waking hours here. So what's it like working in a bar? I always thought that'd be cool." She leaned in a bit. "And I heard the bartenders in this place are hot."

Tessa coughed because she got this a lot. Women who came in alone were notoriously hoping to live out their favorite fantasy—with a good-looking, well-built bartender— and who was she to throw stones? "Saturday night is the night you want to come in. They all work on Saturdays."

"Single?"

"Yes," answered Tessa, withholding the impulse to lie or doctor the truth in some way.

"Which one is that?" asked Marisa, pointing to the picture of Gabe standing next to one of the Knicks cheerleaders.

"That's Gabe. He's the main owner." Tessa then went down the line of photos, needing to point out that Prime had more than one gorgeous bartender on the payroll. "That's his brother Sean next to the mayor's wife. And that's their older brother Daniel ducking out underneath the bar. He doesn't enjoy having his picture taken."

"I like that one," answered Marisa, pointing to Gabe as if she were picking steaks at the butcher.

"He's nice enough," said Tessa, keeping her head down, her eyes glued to the bar.

"Does he have a girlfriend?" continued Marisa, still full of questions, still firmly fixated on Gabe.

"No." Tessa tried not to look encouraging. "He runs the bar and doesn't have a lot of time for relationships."

"Oh." The woman sighed with heavy regret. *Yeah, get over it, sister.* "Still, he's hot. How much time do you really need to have a relationship?"

"Not a lot, apparently."

"Are you friends with him?"

"A little," Tessa replied, neglecting to mention the key facts that she lived with him and was currently sleeping with him, as well. Neither fact would greatly enhance her tip.

"I've got a deal for you. I'll get you into Hudson Towers, you get me a date with your boss."

Marisa, unlike Tessa, was obviously a woman of razor focus and single-minded determination. As luck would have it, object of said razor focus was Gabe, a man whom Tessa didn't want to think she had designs on, yet that cold jab of unease in her stomach called her the world's biggest liar.

"Oh, I don't have that much pull."

Which was the exact moment that Syd chose to enter the conversation.

"Sure she does," he said, nodding in his grizzled-cop manner. One eye squinted knowingly. "Gabe listens to her."

Tessa shook her head at Marisa. "Not really."

"And they're living together, too."

Tessa closed her eyes, wondering what part of "to protect and to serve" the NYPD detective failed to grasp. When she opened her eyes again, she had a perky smile firmly pasted on her face. "Not that way. I'm between roommates at the moment."

"Am I poaching on someone else's reserves?" asked Marisa, wearing a smile on her face that was neither perky nor embarrassed. Tessa felt a momentary pang of envy at such polished composure.

"Oh, no," answered Tessa. "Consider him unpoached. I know Gabe too well to be interested." She turned to Syd and glared meaningfully. "Can I get you a drink?"

"Give me a bourbon since you're not going to let a man have any fun."

Tessa handed him his drink and then waited until he was firmly out of earshot. It was time for Tessa Hart to grow up and stop deluding herself that men were going to take care of her forever. If she wanted something out of life, she was going to have to make choices. This time, unlike seven years ago, she was going to choose what was best for her.

"You really think you could get me into Hudson Towers?"

Marisa looked at her with palpable relief. "They do not call me St. Marisa for nothing."

Tessa took a deep breath. Yes, she loved sleeping with Gabe, but that was meaningless sex—two strangers satisfying a biological urge, nothing more. Tessa needed to remember the personal boundaries, and Marisa was the perfect person to put the boundaries up exactly where they needed to be. Then Tessa could get back on the way to independence and grow some female cojones that had been sorely lacking up to this pitiful juncture in her life.

"I can get you a date with Gabe," she stated firmly, then waited for the obligatory clap of thunder from the heavens or for seven plagues to descend upon Manhattan or for Tessa to be hit by a bus that would suddenly drive through the shadowy plate-glass window. Instead the only thing she got was a pinched nerve in the heart.

Marisa held out a hand over the bar, not sensing the miraculous absence of disaster, nor Tessa's tellingly aching heart. "Tessa, it's been a pleasure doing business with you. For that," she said, pointing to the picture on the wall, "I'll waive my usual commission when you're settled at Hudson Towers."

Tessa smiled tightly, then pointed to Marisa's alcohol-stained suit jacket. "For that, I'll waive the tab."

THE O'SULLIVAN POKER NIGHT was a tradition that first started when Sean needed money to buy his first Harley-Davidson at the age of nineteen. Gabe, who was underage at the time, had welcomed the opportunity to skim off his older brother's beer supply and happily joined in. Daniel, who was an accountant and, ergo, usually took them to the cleaners, saw poker night as the chance to teach his younger brothers fiscal responsibility. But, alas, the lessons were usually unlearned, and Daniel—regretfully—ended up with boatloads of cash.

Gabe liked the quality family time, time spent arguing over rules and in general persecuting his older siblings in whatever way he could. Being the youngest of three boys was tough, and he'd understood a long time ago that if he played fair, he'd lose.

Tonight the beer was flowing and the cards were coming his way. Queens and aces, two pairs and a full house. Daniel seemed to be nursing a run of bad luck, and Sean…well, Sean always lost. Cain was the fourth hand, and he was a tough competitor with a face about as telling as a brick wall. After a couple of hours' play, Gabe was already ahead by a cool hundred.

"Are you sure you're not cheating," asked Sean after losing his three deuces to Gabe's inside straight.

"I don't have to cheat to beat you, Sean. Face it, you suck. This is the main reason you couldn't buy your Harley until after you got your law degree."

Sean didn't look convinced. "Why don't you empty your pockets?"

Gabe would have been insulted if it wasn't a routine they'd acted out for nearly four years.

Daniel, who didn't see the value of family traditions the way that Gabe did, sighed, long and loud.

Cain drummed his chips on the table.

Gabe grinned smugly. "Sure," he told his brother, and pulled out the empty jeans pockets. "Feeling better, counselor? You still suck."

"Boys," interrupted Daniel. "Stop."

Gabe fell silent because Daniel didn't interrupt often.

Gabe passed the deck to Cain, who shuffled and then dealt Gabe a pair of eights, an ace, a two and a five.

Sean looked at his cards, then grinned. He slid out two chips, and then glanced at Gabe. "So tell me about Tessa. How's that working out for you? Getting laid?"

Gabe stared grimly at the cards, keeping his face devoid of anything but extreme interest in poker. "It's Tessa, Sean. Get your mind out of the sewer."

"Not sure if I could handle a woman staring over my shoulder. Got to crimp a man's style—assuming he *has* a style, of course."

Gabe shot him a bite-me look, and Cain stacked his chips into two neat piles. "Are you two going to fight? Because if you are, I want to know so I can keep my money separate."

"They won't fight," answered Daniel.

"I could," snapped Gabe. "Two years ago, you were down, begging for mercy—remember?"

Cain laughed. "Yes, Gabe, we all remember."

"Go ahead, laugh away. I'm the baby here, and I'll take my victories where they come."

Sean grunted, matching Cain's raise and upping it by another ten. Somebody had some sweet cards. "The only reason I let you get that punch in is because Anna Del Toro was watching, and I felt sorry for you in front of your girl. You *are* my baby brother."

"So how *are* you and Tessa getting along?" asked Daniel, casually upping Sean's bet with a rare smile.

"She's usually not here," Gabe said, looking with more doubt at his pair of eights. If Daniel was actually smiling, he was holding something serious.

Cain snickered. "Hard for a man to win a bar pool if you two are never in the same room."

Sean took two cards and didn't try to hide the gleam in his eyes. "Gabe's not getting any. He's too tense. Real shame, too. If you thought about anything but the bar, you'd be a lot happier. Balance. That's what you need. That, and one good night of ball-blasting sex. You're not that bad-looking, and if you worked at it, you'd have women falling all over you. And, by the way, I've got my money on day thirty-one, so if you want to do something really nice for your big brother, arrange a nice romantic dinner for her and maybe a bubble bath."

Gabe rubbed his thumb against the corner of his ace, seriously contemplating the idea of a romantic dinner and a bubble bath with Tessa. It actually wasn't a dumb thought: lathering her up with suds, soaping up the sleek back, the tight thighs.

"Hello? Gabe?" Sean interrupted the momentary fantasy and then shot Daniel a knowing look. "Told you he was suffering. The only person who's going to win the bet is Tessa."

Cain's mouth edged into a small smile. "Tried and struck out?" he asked—and this was from Cain, who usually sided with Gabe. "Sucks, man."

Gabe glared at the two of hearts, trying to will it into another, more worthy card. For instance, another ace. "Contrary to my other, more lecherous brother, I do have a moral conscience."

Sean leaned back in his chair and laughed. "It's a right guaranteed in the Constitution. Life, liberty and the pursuit of—"

"Can we talk about something else?" interrupted Gabe. "Like, for instance, the building permit? Did you find out anything more?"

"Amanda's out of the office until Tuesday next, and I can't

get a straight answer out of the old man that's manning the desk while she's gone."

"But there's no problem with my license, right?"

Sean cracked his knuckles. "Nothing I can't handle, Gabe. Don't worry about a thing."

"Does that mean you'll help me with the work on the expansion while I'm waiting on the permit?"

"No," said Sean, completely without guilt. "But I will help you hire a new bartender to fill said space."

Gabe looked at Daniel in frustration, and Daniel shrugged. No help there. "I'm folding," Gabe announced because he wasn't getting anywhere in cards or logic. Better to quit while he was ahead.

They played in silence until it was nearly midnight, and Gabe kept a close eye on the clock. Tessa would be closing up with Lindy soon, and Gabe wanted to know if her apartment hunting had been successful. Besides that, he didn't feel right about her taking the subway home alone. Tessa would probably hit him if she knew what he was thinking, but Sean was right about one thing: Gabe had a Lancelot complex. And if there was ever a damsel in distress, it was Tessa.

He looked around the table, noticing the pile of money that was now sitting in front of Cain. All right, so he hadn't made his quota. He'd make up for it next week. Then he scrunched up his pain and rubbed two fingers over his temple.

"Can't handle losing?" asked Cain.

"I've been fighting a headache all day. Probably hay fever or something. Listen, I hate to fold up early, but, hell, my head is about to explode."

Gabe gathered up the cards, and Daniel handled the financials. In the end, Gabe was ahead by twenty. Not a bad night's work.

"Same time next week?" asked Cain, pocketing two hundred with a satisfied smile.

"At my place," Sean spoke up.

"Right," agreed Gabe, keeping his head low and headache-looking.

"Why don't you lie down?" suggested Sean. "We know the way out."

Gabe felt a momentary pang of guilt because Sean did actually look concerned, but this was for a good cause. What man in his right mind wouldn't want to make sure that a helpless female got home safely? After all, the streets of New York could be really mean—assuming that you didn't count the FBI reports that said that New York was the safest big city on the planet. But Gabe wasn't a big one for trusting the government stats. Governments lied, and then where would Tessa be? Walking alone on the mean streets of Manhattan.

He managed a weak smile, and then they were gone. Gabe waited another five minutes and then pulled on his boots. Time to get Tessa home.

Gabe remembered the moments in the theater this afternoon, the taste of her neck, the curve of her bare ass and the exquisite cock-raising feeling of being encased in everything that was perfect.

Yeah, this roommate thing wasn't bad at all.

THE NIGHT WASN'T A total loss. Tessa had made over a hundred in tips, and once she had gotten over the initial melancholy of her decision to set up Marisa with Gabe, a peace had come over her. In fact, even Lindy noticed her new attitude when they were cleaning up.

She popped the ice cream into the bar freezer and then stared pointedly at Tessa. "Why are you so pale? Are you getting sick or something?"

"I'm not pale, I feel calm. Collected. I've got a new take-charge attitude, a plan to get into my own place."

"You still look pale," repeated Lindy, shaking her head, and Tessa could feel the melancholy returning.

"To the unknowing eye, perhaps."

With Lindy still looking doubtful, Tessa visualized coming into her perfect apartment surrounded by successful, financially independent colleagues who had made their way in life. As opposed to the pitiful imagery of Tessa dropping out of school, shacking up with Gabe for a couple of years. And then he'd decide he needed a new, improved model, probably someone who had a viable career, and then Tessa would be pushing thirty and still trying to support herself on a bartender's tips. Hudson Towers was looking better and better by the minute.

"So what's the new take-charge attitude from?"

"Taking the hard course, forging ahead with the right decision and following my dreams."

"And this decision has to do with what?"

"The woman that came in here earlier—the one I drenched in vodka? She's going to help me get into Hudson Towers."

"Hudson Towers? All that because you spilled a drink on her? Man, I wish I had your luck. Instead I get stuck with seventeen-year-olds with bad fake IDs who threaten lawsuits and then tell me that the terrorists have won if I report it. Tell me, what does terrorism have to do with underage drinking? I don't get the connection."

Tessa laughed. "What do you want, Lindy?"

"The perfect full-throated orgasm."

"I mean *really*."

Lindy looked askance. "I meant *really*."

"What about Peter?"

Lindy rolled one shoulder forward. "He's only in my mind."

Tessa, who was on a first name basis with the idea of fantasy lovers, nodded with approval. "Sometimes it's better when they're only in your mind."

"As opposed to being only in your vagina?"

Tessa told herself she would not blush, she would not blush, she would not blush.

She blushed.

"Want to spill any secrets?" asked Lindy.

"Nope. Nope, nope, nope."

"Glad somebody is getting something around here." Lindy looked toward the front. "And speak of the devil."

"Hey," answered Gabe, smoothly walking in the door as if he owned the place. Which he did.

Tessa looked at Lindy wide-eyed, terrified and willing thoughts of Hudson Towers back into her feeble brain. "Don't you dare."

Lindy winked. "Not daring at all." Then she waved at Gabe as if everything was right with the world. "Hey, boss."

Gabe headed downstairs, and Lindy finished polishing the beer taps. A moment later she put her hands on her hips, took a long look around and then sighed happily. "I'm off."

"You don't have to leave on my account," said Tessa, not sure she wanted to be alone with Gabe. Actually, she desperately wanted to be alone with Gabe, her weakened flesh already crying to be alone with Gabe. And with Lindy gone? She was toast. Weakened-flesh toast.

"Good night, Tess. And don't do anything I wouldn't do." Lindy added, waving and disappearing into the night.

Leaving Tessa alone. With Gabe.

Actually, she thought, looking around the empty bar. It wasn't so bad. With Gabe downstairs, he was out of visual range, out of touching range, out of kissing range and out of tasting range.

Of course, he took that exact moment to appear. Tessa jumped.

"How did it go with the apartment today?" he asked, a completely casual, logical conversation starter.

"I didn't take it."

"Too small?" he asked, acting completely innocent, completely polite and completely casual.

Tessa stared at him suspiciously. "No, it was huge."

"So what was the problem, Tess?" he prodded, not so innocent anymore, not so polite anymore and—aha—not so carefree anymore, either.

"He has a dog," she answered truthfully.

"You don't like dogs?" he asked.

"They're messy and smelly."

"Right, I didn't know you felt that way. I like cats."

Tessa nodded, picked up a rag and stared rescrubbing the bar sink. A sink could never get too clean. "Yes, yes, I do. Give me a cat any day. Much more suited to apartment living."

"Oh." He stood there, watching her work. "Tessa?" he started, and she could read the soul-searching curiosity in his eyes.

"How was poker night?" she asked, abruptly changing the subject because if there was any soul-searching to be done, it wasn't about to be her soul under the microscope.

Gabe, never obtuse, took the hint. "Lost a bundle. Was doing good at the start, but then Cain came in for the win and started getting the hot hands."

"Sorry."

"Was the place busy tonight? The receipts look good."

"Drenched a customer in vodka," Tessa admitted, happy to be talking about work. Talking about work was good.

Gabe frowned. "He wasn't getting too friendly, was he?"

"It was a she. And, no, it was only me being clumsy."

"You're never clumsy."

Maybe she wasn't clumsy with her hands, but sometimes Tessa was clumsy with her life. "There's a first for everything. Her name was Marisa and she's a Realtor," she started, deciding that now was as good a time as any to fulfill her commitment to set up Marisa with Gabe.

"I bet you two had a lot to talk about. Actually, did you ever think about real estate, Tessa? I think you'd be good at it."

She looked at him and was easily diverted from her match-making goal by the much more interesting idea of pursuing a career in real estate. But *sales?*

However, Gabe looked serious. As if he wasn't joking. As if he thought she could do it. "I think I'd be really bad at it."

"Is that a joke?" he asked.

"No. I can't do sales."

"But when you know what you're doing, it's not like selling, more like…I don't know…finding people and matching them to what they want—and that you could do. Definitely."

"I don't know, Gabe," she started, because she had already decided on a career path and, okay, a D on an accounting test wasn't the most promising of signs, but if she kept changing her path, who knew where she'd end up? Probably a chain-smoker at forty-seven, still tending bar, with a tattoo on her arm that said *Mother* to match the D-E-N-N-Y that was still tattooed on her butt.

"What's the safest apartment building in the city?" asked Gabe.

"The Lucerne," she answered, ripping her mind off the creepy image of a Mother tattoo.

"I'm looking for a building. Pets, walk-up, in Battery Park, and I don't want to pay too much. Where should I start?"

"Liberty Manor," she said automatically, and Gabe gave her one of those annoying I-told-you-so looks.

Slowly it dawned on her that, yes, Gabe was correct. "You think I could do it? I wouldn't, uh, scare people?" she asked, mentally comparing her wine-stained T-shirt to Marisa's un-wrinkled suit.

"Certainly you could do it. But don't quit your night job. I'm not ready to lose my best bartender."

Tessa tossed her rag in his direction. "You're the best bartender here, Gabe."

"I can't put myself in the competition. Wouldn't be fair."

He smiled at her then, looking at Tessa as if she could do anything. And she wanted to believe that.

"Slacker," she teased.

"Speaking of slacker, do you know if they delivered the wood next door?"

"Lindy didn't say anything, but…"

He cocked his head toward the street. "Come on, we'll check it out. You're not in a hurry to get home, are you?"

Home. He said it so easily, and she bought into this whole I-can-live-there-forever fantasy so easily. Still, she shook her head, drifting along, not willing to correct him. "No, I had a cup of coffee at eleven."

"Jeez, you're never getting any sleep tonight."

They walked outside and around the corner to the empty space next door. The early-summer wind was perfect and a soft rain was just starting to fall. Tessa lifted her face to the warm water, feeling herself come alive.

The old bodega had stood vacant for all of two weeks before Gabe had jumped all over it. The truth was, the crowds at Prime did usually bump over capacity, and buying the old space back had been a smart idea. Of course, Gabe was good that way. Making a plan, executing and then seeing it through to success. He didn't wait for anything, or let anything get in his way.

While Tessa watched, he used his keys to lift the grate and then unlock the door.

"We'll have power tomorrow if the gods at Con Ed are agreeable, but tonight darkness rules," he said, as the glass door creaked open.

Tessa followed him through, curious to see the guts of the place now that it was empty. In the darkness there wasn't a lot to see, but even so, she could sense his enthusiasm.

"S'all right," she told him, picking her way around the spools of electrical cable and the mess of tools scattered throughout the place. She stumbled over a power cord, and he caught her arm.

"I've got it," she said and quickly pulled her arm free.

"Sure," he answered, his voice cooling a degree.

Then she noticed the presence of most of telltale cans of Dr Pepper. Gabe was the only person in New York she knew who drank Dr Pepper.

She shook her head, cutting through the dim light to see him standing there, so absolutely sure he could do anything. "And you're going to do this in your spare time?"

"Sure. You can ace accounting, and I can pull a rabbit out of a white Russian."

"You shouldn't believe your own press. Besides, I got a D on my exam last week."

He took a step closer, and she could feel the waves of sympathy emanating from him. Not the pity look—she hated that. "Do you want me to help you study?"

"Accounting?" she asked skeptically.

"Maybe not, but Daniel would if you asked."

"I hate accounting," she said in a quiet voice, sitting down on the electrical spool, confessing the secret that she'd come to realize recently.

He sat down next to her, not touching but exuding that bulk of warming comfort that was fast becoming as necessary to her as water. "Maybe you're chasing the wrong career," he offered gently.

"At some point in time I have to pick one, Gabe. You've known what you've wanted to do since you were sixteen. Not all of us are that lucky."

"Six."

"What?"

"Actually, I've known what I wanted to do since I was six.

Other kids were out playing Starsky and Hutch, me and Sean were inventing drinks and lighting them on fire."

Tessa felt the smile curving her lips. "You're lucky you didn't burn the place down."

"I knew where the fire extinguishers were."

She envied him that sense of belonging, the peace of knowing his future, missing out on the whole what-are-you-going-to-do-with-the-rest-of-your-life? stress. "You really think I could get into real estate?"

"I really think you ought to try if you really want to." His voice had changed, gotten deeper, huskier, and she knew—absolutely knew—that he was bone-stirringly close because her Gabe-challenged nerve endings quivered in response.

In the darkness, she didn't see him move as much as felt it. His hand cupped the back of her neck, unerringly leading her toward his mouth, and—sweet mercy—she wasn't about to pull away.

The tender draw of his lips on hers was something new, not the hot sweat of passion that they'd found before. She tried to conjure up her security blanket of fantasy images. Desperately seeking a handsome stranger who could coax screaming orgasms from her or the dark loner who didn't want anything from her but a single night of sex. But she was losing focus on these men. She wasn't interested in fantasy anymore.

She wanted Gabe.

And if Tessa kept her eye on the sex only, not letting her heart get involved, not getting distracted from her goals, she could have her cake and eat it, too.

Sex. That's all she had to focus on. The sex. And it wasn't difficult because, well, she knew about sex with Gabe and, best of all, she loved the sex with Gabe.

Unfortunately, Gabe wasn't in on her plan. His kiss was no promise of raw sex but a promise of something else. Tessa grew bold, shifting in his lap, trying to turn the kiss back into sex, but Gabe seemed unusually determined now.

When she pushed her hand down between them, working to cup his erection, he took her hand quite firmly and placed it behind her back. When she gently bit his lower lip, pulling it between her teeth, he laughed.

Gabe leaned into her, and she could feel the hammering of his heartbeat against hers. The pulse of the heart wasn't what she needed to concentrate on, she needed to focus on the pulse between her thighs. The pulse between his thighs.

Tessa pushed her hips closer, not so subtly telling him what she wanted.

His lips nuzzled the side of her neck, coaxing a moan from her. "Do you know who I am, Tess?"

The words were so husky, so pressing, so seductive, and she could hear his name echoing in her head, but she wasn't going to do this. She already had one man's name tattooed on her skin, a burning reminder of how far she still had to go until she could take care of herself. It was important that she keep the distance between them until it was time. Until she had built a life of her own. She trusted Gabe with pretty much everything but not the future. She trusted no man with her future.

Did she know who he was? "No," she lied.

He laughed again, low, and this time one hand curved under her shirt, palming one breast, feeling the rise of her nipples, the swell of her flesh.

She arched into him, pushing her skin more firmly in his hand, needing the hot touch. He lifted her shirt, replacing his hand with his mouth, biting gently.

The ache between her thighs pounded now, and she could feel her resolve melting. Anything—anything—to fill the ache inside her.

"Do you know who I am, Tessa?"

"No," she snapped, the knot of frustration winding tighter and tighter. And the desire, too. Always the desire.

This time his wayward hand went farther, unzipping her jeans, sliding down, lower, until one finger stroked against her core. Tessa cried out because this teasing wasn't enough.

"Who am I, Tessa?" he asked, his voice rough, but still so familiar.

"No," she answered because she needed the defenses between them. The one tiny wall remaining was all that was keeping her from falling down on her knees and giving up everything that she wanted.

Quietly, in the darkness, he removed his hands from her, zipped up her jeans and adjusted her shirt.

Tessa sat on the wooden spool, her body still shaking and tense, waiting for him to return.

"Please," she started, needing him to finish, needing him inside her.

Needing Gabe.

She felt his gaze in the shadows, could nearly touch the cold snap of his anger. And his voice, when it sounded, was crystal clear.

"No."

7

GABE MET SEAN FOR racquetball on Friday morning. Playing racquetball with Sean was usually a pain in the ass, but in the end Gabe had agreed because he had to talk to somebody about Tessa. Slowly, quietly, painfully, Gabe was going insane.

The challenge here was that Gabe would have to talk about Tessa in a way that Sean wouldn't know Gabe was talking about Tessa, but Gabe figured he could handle that. He had to.

All due to this damned need of hers to pretend that Gabe wasn't Gabe.

Yes, at first he'd thought it was hot. Every guy likes to think that his girl has an active fantasy life.

But every time? That sad truth wears a man down.

So on Friday morning he was stuck in Sean's high-end athletic club, which was filled with white-collar alpha males needing to assert their masculine superiority in a twenty-by-twenty room with no windows.

Gabe dressed in cutoffs and an FDNY Engine 31 T-shirt, which was his token effort to assert masculine superiority. He took in Sean's tennis whites, and arched a mocking eyebrow. "I think I should call you Mortimer or Preston or something equally nerdy."

Sean shook his head and pointed to the court. "Hello, my name is Sean O'Sullivan. You mock my clothes. Prepare to die."

Gabe followed him inside, slammed the door closed. Next

he lifted his racquet, gave a cursory bow to his opponent— and then, the war was on.

Gabe took the first game fifteen to eleven. Sean came back, perfecting his killer smash, and took the second game fifteen to seven.

By the third game they were both sweating like pigs, and the game had regressed to a primitive slog to the death. Never let it be said that an O'Sullivan wasn't competitive. One long hour later Sean took the match fifteen to thirteen. Gabe didn't mind because this felt good. Relaxed. Powerful. And his mind was completely Tessa-free.

Progress, definitely progress.

Besides, he'd whip his brother's ass the next time. There was always a next time.

They showered, changed, and Sean bought a drink for Gabe at the juice bar. Gabe ducked his head low in case anybody recognized him. He had a reputation to uphold, and sipping soy juice at some Nancy-boy health bar wasn't part of it.

Only for Tessa—and she would never know the depths he had sunk to in order to keep this Twilight Zone of a relationship alive.

When the bartender shoved the glass of OJ in Gabe's direction, Gabe sniffed and then raised his glass. "To my brother, who has fallen far, far from the esteemed ideals that the O'Sullivan name has stood for through four generations. Juice? *Juice?* What is this?"

"I think it's important to maintain a healthy lifestyle. Alcohol can be dangerous," Sean said, pushing back the hair from his eyes, trying to weasel his way into respectability.

"Sean, our family's fortune was made on the ill-gotten gains of illegal alcohol. O'Sullivan's started as a speakeasy. You can run to a career in the law, but you can't hide."

"That doesn't mean we can't go straight."

Gabe downed the juice in one gulp. "Are you sure we're related? You're the brown-eyed kid. Why brown? Did you ever think about that, Sean?"

"Why are you here?" asked Sean, sipping demurely at his carrot juice.

Carrot juice? Gabe sighed, wanting to avoid this, but he couldn't. This was important. And if he had to humiliate himself in front of his lesser-respected brother, then so be it. "I need to talk to you about a woman. You are still interested in women, aren't you?"

Sean laughed and appeared relieved by the change of subject, the flicker of humanity coming back into his eyes. "Desperate, aren't you? Coming to the master."

"Don't rub it in, this is hard enough. I can't talk to Daniel, because I can't handle talking to Daniel about sex. That'd be cruel. I'm not cruel."

Sean tugged at the cuffs of his Brooks Brothers shirt and studied Gabe like a scientist. "So we're actually having sex with this female? Are you sure this isn't a case of lusting from afar?"

At that moment Gabe wished he had a tie. Something silky, probably with a designer label. Preferably long enough that he could loop it around his brother's neck and then pull. Tightly. He smiled at the thought.

"No, it's not lusting from afar. But it would be a lot easier."

"That's just sad, Gabe."

"Yes, yes, it is." He took a deep breath and pitched his voice low, finally admitting the unsavory truth. "She likes to pretend, Sean."

"Pretend what?"

"Pretend that I'm not me."

Sean stroked his chin. "I see. So she's so revolted by you that she has to pretend you're someone else."

"That's not it," Gabe snapped and saw heads turn with curiosity. He scowled back.

"It looks like it. Why else would she need to pretend? Unless you can't satisfy her, of course."

"Of course I can satisfy her," answered Gabe through gritted teeth.

"On the basis of the facts as presented before me, I'm thinking that answer is a big no."

"Screw you, Sean."

Sean lifted his hands. "Okay, okay. All joking aside, I can see you're in need of guidance. Did you ever think about ditching her?"

The bartender came over, clearing the glasses. "Another round of juice?"

"Not in this lifetime," said Gabe. He glared at his brother, feeling uncomfortable. "Hell, a man needs a BlackBerry and a cellphone in order to fit in here. Next time, we're playing wall ball the old-fashioned way—out in the alley."

"Sure, if it makes you feel better. But I'll still whip your ass. Now, getting back to the sex girl—which is much more interesting than how I can wipe the floor with you—why don't you ditch her? You're not the obsessive-compulsive type."

"I can't ditch her," answered Gabe, sounding obsessively compulsive.

"Why? Every woman can be ditched for the right reasons."

"I like her. I'm not going to stop seeing her."

A big guy in sweats plopped down next to Sean and started talking, completely butting into a personal conversation. Gabe sat for a few minutes while Sean chatted legal gibberish with the other dude until Gabe cleared his throat.

"Do you mind?" he asked Sean.

Sean turned to the other guy. "My little brother. He needs help. Sorry."

The man held out his hand. "You're Daniel? I'm Frankie Ryder. How you doing?"

"No, I'm Gabe," he responded, shaking the meaty paw but shooting meaningful "hurry-up" glances to Sean.

Frankie turned to Sean. "I didn't know you had two brothers."

"I'm the brother he keeps hidden up in the attic."

"Gabe, you don't have to be rude." Sean looked at Frankie. "He's a little edgy. It's a sex thing."

"Excuse me?" Gabe coughed.

Frankie blushed around the gills and then sat up. "I'll see you back at the office, Sean."

"Sure thing," said Sean with a happy wave.

"Did you need to drag this out in the open?"

"No, but it seemed like the fun thing to do. And stop acting like you're the only man in the world who's ever suffered from blue balls. Do you know that ninety-nine-point-seven-three percent of men's frustrations come from sex issues? If I didn't tell Frankie, he'd figure it out. One of the best estate lawyers this side of hell. Great guy."

"I'm sure Frankie's great, but can we get back to my problems?"

"Ah, so now you do want to admit you have a problem? Which is an important step because, yes, you do—a giant one. Why do you think she has to pretend?" asked Sean, using his courtroom cross-examination voice, but Gabe was too wound up to care.

Wasn't *that* the million-dollar question? Gabe had thought long and hard about why, but he couldn't come up with anything. "I don't know why. There doesn't have to be a *why*. Why *why?* I don't want to think about *why*."

"Why goes to motive, Gabe."

"This isn't a court case. I'm talking sex. Just sex."

"But don't you want to know her *why?*"

"No, I only want to fix it."

"What if you can't?"

"Can't? What does that mean?"

"What if she can never accept you for who you are or for what you are? Maybe she has issues with dating a bartender? Maybe, for instance, she's always wanted a more cerebral man. Like me."

"It's not that."

"So you do know the *why.*"

"I don't care about the *why.*"

"Then there's your problem. She has a *why,* you don't care about the *why* and she wants you to care about the *why.* Elementary, Gabe, elementary. You just have to understand the female psyche."

Gabe looked around the club, seeing it through the red haze of his rage. "This is pointless. I shouldn't have talked to you."

"Why don't you talk to Tessa?"

Gabe pretended he wasn't affected, but, okay, his heart stopped for a second. "What? What do you mean?"

Sean looked completely casual. "Tessa. A female point of view, who conveniently happens to be your roommate, as well. Maybe she can explain the *why.*"

Gabe hid his sigh of relief. "I'm not sure that Tessa is the right person to talk to."

"Why?" asked Sean, his eyes narrowed—and suspicious.

Quickly Gabe backed off. "You're right. I'll talk to Tessa. I bet she'll know exactly what to do."

Sean grinned. "See? Look how smart your older brother is."

People didn't realize how difficult it was being the youngest of three brothers. People didn't give Gabe enough credit for putting up with bullshit like this.

However, Gabe rose above all the crap that Sean dished out. He was the bigger man. "You're lucky this time, Sean. Next time, I'm going to smash your candy ass into the floor."

"Empty threats, nothing more. Because it's obvious that I'm the lover in the family, baby brother, as well as the fighter."

Gabe eyed the silk tie around his brother's neck, considered the very real presence of witnesses, and opted to spare Sean's life. But only because Sean was wrong. Gabe was the lover in the family.

Sean signaled the bartender, and he came over holding the glasses in his hand completely wrong. *Poser.*

"Another round of juice."

"Just the check. Sean's paying." Gabe slapped his brother on the back. "Thanks, bro."

Then he left this godforsaken establishment before its wholesome aura started to rub off on him.

Carrot juice? Jeez.

TESSA SPENT THURSDAY afternoon looking at apartments and meeting potential roommates. Some people might call it boring, Tessa considered it depressing. She'd met Stella, a longtime bartender at 87 Park, who was a fifty-three-year-old with platinum blond hair and a rose tattoo on her arm and, best of all, she smoked like a chimney. Tessa mentally did the math. Fifty-three minus twenty-six was twenty-seven. Tessa had twenty-seven years before she ended up like Stella—not that there was anything wrong with that.

But Tessa wanted more.

After Stella there'd been Barry, who was twenty-two, and just starting in the MBA program at Columbia. After ten minutes in the shadow of his type-A personality, Tessa knew she would turn suicidal.

After Barry, there'd been Karen, who was an aspiring Broadway dancer. Everything was fine until Tessa had met Karen's fiancé, Chaz, who'd slapped Tessa on the butt immediately after meeting her, and then started talking threesomes when Karen went to answer her phone. Tessa hadn't waited for Karen to get back.

Next Tessa had gone up to Washington Heights, crossed over to the Bronx and then gone south to Bensonhurst. She'd seen studios, one-bedrooms and lofts—and exactly zero that she wanted to live in. The studios were like living in a closet. The first one-bedroom she'd seen had a view over the sanitation facility, the second was directly over the subway, shaking ominously every ten to twelve minutes. And the loft was not even in the same area code of her price range.

All in all, it was true: in the naked city, there was only one building that provided good value and adequate security.

Hudson Towers. Someday maybe the New York real estate market would go bust—possibly Tessa's great-great-grandchildren would see it—but not anytime before.

For a second she considered moving, moving back to Florida, giving up, telegraphing to the world that, yes, it was true, Tessa couldn't survive on her own.

Only one second did she consider this defeatist mentality. No way. No way in hell.

Marisa wouldn't give up. Marisa would take the deal and not lose any sleep.

That was the thing about people like Marisa. They were connected, knew people who knew people and made it their business to make sure they were always collecting more people.

Marisa wanted to add Tessa to her collection and she wanted to add Gabe, as well. Quid pro quo. The world ran on quid pro quo.

The answer was simple.

Tessa would get her apartment, she'd help out Marisa, and she'd get over this Gabe thing. It was a sexual crush, nothing more. She'd been too long without a man and he'd been the first guy in four years, so it was completely natural that she was a little overheated.

But passion didn't last. Not like real estate.

No, her apartment was her future. The men would have to wait their turn because Tessa was going to get her own place, pay her own bills, buy her own furniture and possibly get a cat.

Friday afternoon was her accounting class, so she went and

listened to Professor Lewis drone on about tangible operational assets and intangible operational assets, which helped cement her own operational decision.

Gabe was right. Accounting was a mistake. She'd just picked a career out of the phone book instead of trying to figure out what she wanted to do with the rest of her life. However, to be fair, she'd never had to pick out a career before, and who knew there was a right way and a wrong way to do it?

Well, lesson learned. Considering she had to execute an alternate career plan, like, yesterday she was going to talk to Marisa ASAP. Immediately after class she pulled out the Realtor's wrinkled card and punched the numbers on her cell.

"Marisa—Tessa. The bartender from Prime? How you doing?"

"Good. I didn't expect to hear from you so soon. Wow, you work fast."

Unfortunately Marisa wasn't interested in Tessa's life decision. No, she wanted to talk about men in general, Gabe in particular.

Shoot.

"Actually, I want to talk to you about something else. Can you meet me for a drink? Or dinner—I don't care. I need to ask you a few questions."

"About Gabe?"

"Yeah," answered Tessa. "Yeah."

"Sounds great. I'll meet you at that new bar on the corner of Bleecker and Grover."

Tessa knew the place. Chrome, black, cute little colored lights, yet pretentious and expensive, with watered-down drinks. Okay, fine, whatever.

Forty-five minutes later Tessa changed into her best pair of black jeans and dashed into Century 21 to buy a dressier shirt. Attire was something she'd never worried about before, but now appearances mattered. The golden, glittery top looked great in the dressing room, but the frumpy haircut? Tessa glared at her own reflection in the mirror and sighed. She could fix clothes, but hair couldn't be fixed in ten minutes. Actually, it could, but even Tessa knew that getting a haircut in ten minutes or less was a really bad idea. She'd done that once when she was seventeen. Not doing that again. Later, when she had the time, she would fix the hair thing.

When she got to the club, she scoured the room for Marisa, finally spotting her near the back, dressed exquisitely in some neatly pressed olive-green suit that brought out the highlights in Marisa's exquisitely styled hair.

Marisa, to her credit, looked over Tessa's new, improved wardrobe and didn't say a word.

No, the first words out of her mouth were, "Did you talk to him?"

Tessa, whose last conversation with Gabe had consisted of very little communication, having more to do with groping and grabbing, elected to spin the truth. "The time wasn't exactly right."

Marisa looked disappointed.

Tessa realized that disappointment wasn't how you approached the sole person who could help you on this new career in real estate. "But there'll be more chances," she added, throwing in an optimistic smile.

Marisa perked up nicely. "I checked into Hudson Towers for you. I know a guy who knows a guy who has an aunt who's about to move into assisted living. Her place is going up for sublet in another three weeks. I gave him your name, and he was excited to avoid the whole finding-a-new-renter nonsense. How's that for results?"

Holy moley. In another three weeks she'd have her ideal place. Solo. Marisa was faster than most cabdrivers Tessa had ridden with. "Really? You're not just yanking my chain, are you?"

"Cross my heart," promised Marisa.

Tessa ordered a drink from the waitress, choosing to stick to a diet soda. Better to maintain a clear head tonight. After all, this was business. Marisa, not knowing that tonight was business, ordered a Tom Collins.

"When did you decide to go into apartment rentals?" Tessa asked after the waitress deposited their drinks.

Marisa tossed back the hair from her face in one very confident, self-assured flick. "I futzed around after college, trying to design an interesting career around a degree in liberal arts, and then I realized that this city lived and breathed real estate. I didn't have to teach English if the possibility gave me hives. I could do something more exciting, and financially a lot more rewarding."

A degree. Bummer. But Tessa wasn't discouraged yet. "But somebody wouldn't have to have a degree, would they?"

Marisa shook her head. "Oh, no. We have this one kid in the office who's fifteen, and even though legally he can't act as an agent, he's as good as a walking database of New York City apartments. When he turns eighteen, he'll be earning a fortune."

"Wow. Fifteen," murmured Tessa, shamed by a mere fifteen year old with more business sense than her. "I want to go into real estate, Marisa. I know more about the apartments in this city than anybody, even your fifteen-year-old whiz kid." There. She'd done it. She'd actually tried to sell herself.

"Really?" asked Marisa, which was better than *Get out of my face, bitch, you're bothering me.*

Tessa was mildly encouraged. "Sure, test me."

And for the next half hour Marisa did. Tessa knocked off the answers one by one, not hesitating, her confidence growing by leaps and bounds.

Eventually Marisa sat back in her chair, arms crossed across her chest. And there was approval on her face. Actual

Tessa approval. "You do know your stuff. You think you can handle the exam?"

"With flying colors," answered Tessa, getting cockier by the millisecond, so close to Hudson Towers she could taste it.

"There's a weeklong course that you'll have to take. And then pass the exam. But, yeah, I'd vouch for you."

And, yes, success. Tessa was in.

"Thank you for all your help."

Marisa smiled graciously. "Not a problem. You're helping me out, too," she reminded Tessa.

"I can't believe you have problems meeting men." Because Tessa could see the guys in the club checking out Marisa.

"I'm tired of stuffy Manhattan studs who think every woman must fall down at their feet and perform full-throated fellatio within thirty seconds of the first meet and greet. I'd rather find someone who can respect me. What I like about bartenders is that they seem to respect females. It's a very therapeutic profession."

"Yeah, I've heard that," Tessa replied.

Marisa leaned her chin on her palm. "Tell me about Gabe."

Gabe? Did they really have to talk about Gabe? Yes, apparently they did.

Tessa, not quite willing to give up yet, looked around wildly, her eyes resting on the surfer boy who was tending to the bar. "What about this guy? He looks sensitive, almost poetic. I bet he'd love to go out with you."

"Nah. We dated a few months ago and I broke up with him. I think he was still hung up on his ex-girlfriend or something. You know, it's very hard for men to break free from repressed memories."

Oh, man. Marisa was about forty thousand steps ahead of Tessa in the relationship world. "What about the bartenders at Club X? I knew this one bartender there—we played against them in softball last year—and he was fabulous. The most perfect set of abs you've ever seen."

"Mario?"

"Oh." Tessa's face fell. "You know him."

"Yeah," answered Marisa. "We didn't go out, though. He's got a bad track record of date-'n'-dump. I don't need that."

"You really know your bartenders, don't you?" said Tessa, trying to get used to the very real possibility of Marisa dating Gabe. He would be impressed with Marisa. She was confident, successful, nice, well put together and she really liked her bartenders.

"A woman can't be too careful in this city."

"No," Tessa chimed in. Quickly she ordered a shot of tequila, deciding that the vision of Gabe and Marisa was best seen through alcohol-tinted glasses. "A woman can't."

The waitress brought two shooters and Tessa clinked her glass with Marisa's. "To my hookup with Hudson Towers."

Marisa grinned. "To my hookup with Gabe O'Sullivan."

The pale liquid should have been hemlock. But as Marisa had said, a woman couldn't be too careful in this city.

Tessa launched the tequila down her throat. Time to get off the Gabe train while she still could. It'd be too easy to fall back into the same depend-on-a-man trap and get sidetracked from learning to take care of herself. Tessa had dreams, and it was time to start fulfilling them. It was time to either put up or shut up. Either Tessa could take care of herself or else she was going to end up like Stella or with a boyfriend like Chaz who would want to sleep with Tessa's friends—all at the same time.

No way. Not Tessa. She was going to do this.

No more sex. No more sex at all.

WHEN GABE CAME HOME at two in the morning, Tessa was sacked out on the couch, his old throw cuddled in her arms.

The TV was tuned to MSNBC, which gave him a short pause, but he turned it off anyway.

A book was tucked underneath the throw—"New York State Real Estate Requirements"—and he noticed Tessa's accounting book lying suspiciously next to the trash. There was a new wind blowing, and Tessa wasn't wasting any time.

Gabe watched her sleep, then shook his head. Damned if he'd leave her on the couch all night, so he gathered her up in his arms, happy when she curled into his chest as though she belonged there.

Carefully he carried her to her bed, wishing she'd picked out something nicer than the futon. If he didn't think she'd have a heart attack, he'd move her into his room, but Tessa had her whole personal-boundaries issues, and he was going to respect them.

Actually, Gabe wanted to see Tessa make it. For four years he'd watched her press forward, her forehead worried into one long line that even BOTOX couldn't fix, but she kept going on, roommate after roommate, roadblock after roadblock, never asking for help, never complaining. The little bartender that could—that was her.

Gabe gave her a quick kiss on the forehead, smoothing the lines of worry away.

She was complicated, irrational, skittish…and completely irresistible.

So it'd be complicated. So what? Gabe gave her a long look and then snuck out, closing the door behind him.

Yeah, he'd respect her personal boundaries, but that didn't mean he couldn't seduce her personal boundaries right out of the equation.

In fact, it'd be his pleasure.

DANIEL O'SULLIVAN WASN'T a man to complain, but by the time he interviewed the fifth of Sean's candidates for the new bartender position he decided to forget tradition and raise holy hell.

The blonde was cheerful, flirty, and didn't know whiskey from vodka. However, she did have breasts that torpedoed out from here to eternity.

Daniel sighed, told the woman to have a nice day, and then went downstairs to the office. This was Prime, not Hooters, and he'd be damned if he would spend a perfectly good Saturday afternoon wasting his time, although, to be fair, it wasn't as if he had anything better to do than waste his time. Daniel had become very good at wasting time.

Meanwhile, Sean was sitting at the desk playing solitaire on the bar's computer. Wasting time seemed to be an O'Sullivan family trait.

"What are are you doing?"

Sean turned and quickly clicked over to a spreadsheet. "What do you think? She's great, isn't she?"

Daniel could feel the start of a world-class headache.

"Stop coming up with candidates to interview, will you? This isn't your own personal casting couch."

"You could make it yours. It'd probably improve your disposition." Sadly, Sean was completely serious.

"That's your answer to everything, isn't it, Sean?"

"It's not my fault I'm a people person. I bet you didn't know that lately people have been coming to me for advice, and I've discovered a new talent. Giving personal advice. You know, people come to me as a lawyer all the time. Why not come to me as a personal advisor? The best part? I don't charge by the hour."

"What idiot comes to you for personal advice?"

"Our younger brother is having sexual difficulties. But you wouldn't notice, would you?"

"Gabe?" asked Daniel, too shocked to doubt the truth of the matter.

Sean nodded. "He's having women problems."

Gabe? Women? Hell, Daniel would be having women problems before Gabe. Gabe was grounded, levelheaded, knew what he wanted and didn't waste anybody's time. Gabe didn't have problems, period. "I don't believe you."

"Ask him."

"For real?" asked Daniel, only because Sean didn't have the little gleam in his eyes that he got when he was lying.

"Yeah. Pitiful."

Daniel listened as Sean filled him in on the details, until eventually his curiosity overcame the need to respect his brother's privacy. "Who is she?"

"Some woman he picked up."

"Did he say that?" asked Daniel, because Gabe didn't pick up women. They tried to pick him up, and he always said no. Well, almost always. For the past four years Gabe had barely looked at women at all.

Except for one.

It had become something of an inside joke to Daniel, watching Gabe and Tessa together—and yet not. In some ways, Daniel was living vicariously through his younger brother, remembering what it felt like. That smile when she walked into the room, the easy comfort of knowing that there was always someone waiting for you at home.

There was never any overt sexual tension between Tessa and Gabe—they were too casual for that. It took a detail man to notice the way they got along so easily, knowing what the other one needed before asking, laughing at jokes that no one else got. And then there was the way Gabe protected Tessa, making sure the problem customers were never sitting at her bar. Looking out for her when she was shorthanded and in general making sure that Tessa didn't hurt.

Daniel understood that. Understood the idea that there was

only one woman created exactly, specifically for each man. Life was very precise, as was love.

Fate had decreed that they be together. Maybe it wasn't fate, maybe it was God. Daniel believed in both.

Eight years ago Daniel had found Michelle, loved her to the exclusion of every other female on the planet—and in a single moment God took her away.

But Gabe still had his moment. He had an entire lifetime to celebrate the exact, specific woman who was created perfectly for him.

Daniel looked up at the betting pool. Saw the neatly written numbers and the names next to them and then laughed out loud.

"What's so funny?" demanded Sean.

"You wouldn't understand," replied Daniel. Sean wouldn't get it. For Sean, sex was the be-all and end-all to women.

And to prove Daniel's point, Sean pulled out an application from the pile. "Whatever, but let's talk bartenders for a moment, shall we? This is Leslie, and she's got this long, long, dark hair, and the woman is ready, willing and completely bedworthy. I think she'd be great. Really."

ON SATURDAY MORNING Tessa emerged from her bedroom in a Grateful Dead T-shirt that skimmed her knees.

Gabe looked up from the *Post,* not wanting to imagine what was under the T-shirt, and if he wasn't going to imagine what was under there, he needed to make sure she couldn't read it on his face.

"So how was last night?" he asked.

Tessa padded over to the cabinets, and pulled out a box of cereal, then seated herself at the table next to him. "Fun," she answered, taking a handful of cereal and popping it into her mouth like candy.

"And class?"

She stopped crunching, and then swallowed. "Not fun. I'm quitting."

And wasn't that about time? "New plans?"

"Yeah. Real estate. I've been talking to a friend. There's a class starting in the middle of next week. I'm signing up."

"You have enough money to cover the cost?" Knowing Tessa, she'd live on ramen noodles and cereal before she'd take any help.

"Oh, yeah." Her hand reached into the box again. "You should meet this girl. Marisa. The one who's been helping me. She's completely cool. I think you'd like her."

"Probably not," Gabe responded, not wanting to state out loud that his attention was currently occupied but wondering why Tessa couldn't figure this out on her own. In terms of life issues, maybe she was directionally challenged, but she wasn't dense. At least not usually.

She folded up the bag of cereal, her mouth fixed in a solemn line. "I've been thinking."

Never good, but Gabe wasn't worried. Quickly he directed the conversation to the one he wanted. "Sounds like you've got a lot to think about. A career change, a roommate search. I'm glad you're thinking." There, positive affirmations. The perfect way to get women to do what you wanted them to.

But when she met his eyes, he saw sadness there. Oh, this really wasn't going to be good.

"I don't think I can sleep with you anymore," she said.

Aha, maybe not so bad. So she'd come to see the error of the strange relationship they had? "Actually, I'm glad you think that way. I want to change things around, too."

"You do?"

Honesty. He'd avoided talking because he knew it would scare her, but since she'd brought it up… "Yeah. I don't like this, Tessa. I want us to go out. We don't have to tell anybody. I don't think that'd be a good idea—it's too soon, and people will interfere and get in the way. But I want us to be normal. Don't get me wrong here, I love having sex with you, but it bugs me because I feel like I'm taking advantage of you because of you living here and working at the bar, and I don't like that. As a rule, I don't handle guilt well."

Tessa frowned. "I don't think you understand."

Of course he understood. Out of the entire universe of people, Gabe was the only one who was practicing common sense. However, not the time. It couldn't be possible that Sean was right. Maybe Tessa just wanted him to try and understand her.

"Then help me understand. What do I need to understand?" Gabe asked.

"I can't sleep with you at all. I can't go out with you. It's getting in the way."

Gabe put down the paper, now giving her his undivided attention. This conversation wasn't nearly as easy as he'd thought it would be. "Getting in the way? It doesn't have to get in the way. You need time to study—I can respect that. In fact, I think I've been awesome at trying to not get in your way."

"I can't do this," she told him quietly.

"Why?" Gabe asked, really starting to hate that word.

"I don't know why."

"There's got to be a why, Tessa. This is me. Gabe. You can tell me anything." Damn, his voice sounded desperate. Gabe didn't like desperate.

Tessa pulled back. He saw her pull back physically and knew she had pulled back emotionally, as well. "There is no *why.* I just decided that it's not smart. There. *Not smart.* That's my *why.* It's time that I started being smart, Gabe."

"You are smart," he spoke up automatically.

"Not smart enough. If I were smarter, I would know people. I would have a career plan. I wouldn't have to depend on my friends for my living quarters."

Gabe opened his mouth, then closed it. He couldn't believe the nonsense that was coming out of her. It was as if she was turning into some completely new person, and Gabe didn't like it. He wanted the old Tessa back.

"I'm more than your friend, Tessa."

"No, Gabe. No, you're not," she said, the ultimate knife in the back.

He looked into her eyes, trying to read her mind, trying to see the things that he had always grasped so easily before. There was no freaking way that Gabe had misread this situation, and Tessa seemed ready to cry.

"You don't mean that."

She nodded, her lips pursed tightly together.

"You don't want this?" Gabe asked, still waiting for her to tell him the truth. But they were good together. In fact, they were better than good together.

"I can't want this," she stated slowly, with a dignity that was usually lacking from her words.

Gabe rose up from the table, needing to stop looking at her. He wanted to hit out, yell, make her come to her senses, but that wouldn't accomplish anything at all.

"Fine," he answered and walked to his room, slamming the door.

Even if it hurt him.

He wanted to ignore her, pretend she didn't exist, let the anger cool. But goddamn—

Tessa was his roommate.

Goddamn.

THE REST OF THE AFTERNOON was a milder form of hell for Tessa. She spent the afternoon locked in her room. Not that locks were necessary—Gabe wasn't coming anywhere near her. Her feminine intuition told her that truth. Her feminine intuition, along with the raging chaos in Gabe's eyes.

He left for the bar around two, slamming the door behind him, probably being polite and letting her know he was leaving.

Tessa immediately burst into tears.

And this from two people who weren't, as a rule, emotional.

Okay, this hadn't gone as she'd planned. Tessa had thought she could be mature and able to handle the ending of a relationship—using the term *relationship* loosely—without feeling as if the floor had been pulled out from underneath her.

Sadly Gabe was the foundation she'd built the last four years on, and now she knew that foundation was gone.

And where had that come from? For four years she'd worked her butt off to get her own place in New York. And now it was right within her grasp, but her priorities were getting all whacked. All because of sex with Gabe. Tessa wanted Gabe, but she wanted to have things the way they were—but she knew there was no going back. She'd known that from the first time he'd kissed her when that lightning bolt of awareness shot through her and made her open her eyes to feelings she had never wanted to admit. She depended on Gabe too much. He was her boss, her roommate and, most of all, her friend. But seeing a guy naked complicated things, and aching to have him inside you killed all that friendship stuff in a heartbeat.

Tessa sniffed away the last of her tears. Tears were for losers, and Tessa wasn't a loser. She was a survivor and she could get through this, as well.

She showered and dressed for work, not thinking about the big hole in her chest. All she needed to do was pull on her big-girl panties because right now she had a job to do.

At the bar, the regulars were lined up in front of Gabe, exactly as if everything were normal.

Tessa pasted her usual smile on her face because, yes, this was normal. Completely normal. She didn't need to feel as if she'd been doused over the head with a bucket of ice.

Gabe flashed her a smile, not really so normal, more like "mad as hell, but we'll pretend," and Tessa looked down, concentrating on cutting lemons.

Thankfully the weather outside was sunny and fabulous, and so the crowds started pouring in early, which didn't give her much time to dwell on her own misery. In fact, after a few hours, things did start to seem normal. When the tap went dry, Gabe was there to tap the new one for her. When a very forward slut-puppy began hitting on Gabe, Tessa sent Lindy over to rescue him by pretending to be his girlfriend. When Sean took an extended break with some redhead, Tessa filled in smoothly, covering two of the three bars without a misstep. It wasn't the Paris Peace Accord, but it wasn't World War III either. When Sean returned to the bar, slightly out of breath and flushed, Gabe didn't even seem to mind.

Tessa had made it past depressed and was halfway to optimistic when Marisa breezed in, a vision in bright blue silk, turning all male heads in her path.

Except for Gabe's.

Marisa shouldered through to find a seat in front of Tessa. "How's it going?"

"Busy," answered Tessa, which she hoped would prevent long, extended Gabe-filled conversations.

"Were you able to talk to him? Should I go introduce myself? Do you think this dress is okay? Not too trashy? I wanted sexy but classy. This is sexy but classy, don't you think?"

Tessa stared, unable to reconcile this babbling sinkhole of female insecurities with confident, self-assured Marisa. However, it did make her feel more comfortable with her own lack of confidence when it came to Gabe. Did he affect all women this way? Probably.

Tessa smiled at Marisa, somewhat vindicated. "You look great. Don't worry. I started laying the groundwork for you, but let me go over and say a few more things, and then you sit at his bar for a while. Oh, and one thing—I didn't tell him about the apartment at Hudson Towers. He never liked the place, and I don't want to say anything. Let's keep that part just between us. Okay?"

Marisa nodded. "Sure. You'll talk to him now?"

Tessa nodded and wiped suddenly sweaty palms on her rag. She could do this. She could definitely do this. She tightened her smile, took a deep breath and went to see Gabe.

He was pouring a pitcher of beer and he looked up, surprised to see her.

"Everything okay?" he asked.

Tessa nodded. "You remember me talking to you about Marisa, the Realtor who's getting me into school?"

"Yeah," he said, looking at her, confused.

Not that she could blame him. She knew everything that was going on and she still felt confused. "I think you should talk to her. Get to know her. I think you two would really hit it off."

"Leave it alone, Tessa. I'm not feeling friendly." He sloshed the pitcher on the bar, which was a testament to how unfriendly he was currently feeling. Gabe didn't slosh. Ever.

Tessa flashed Marisa a reassuring smile and turned back to Gabe.

"She's very pretty. And she's nice, too."

"What is with you?" he asked.

"Nothing," she said, licking suddenly dry lips.

"You're hell-bent on setting me up with her, aren't you?"

"Yes."

"Why?"

"Because I like her and I like you, and I think you two would get along well," replied Tessa. She wasn't the world's greatest actress, but man, she should really get an award for this…assuming she could walk away from Gabe without bursting into tears—again.

Gabe wasn't buying it, wasn't even close to buying it, but at least he had stopped asking why.

"Send her over. I'll make sure she has a great time," he snapped, which sounded more like a threat.

Tessa walked away because, yes, she was going to fall apart here, and there were over one hundred thirsty customers and they all needed her.

She squared her shoulders, tightened her stomach and swore to herself that as soon as she was alone she could fall apart. But not until then.

Tessa was getting stronger.

GABE FELT AS IF HE had walked onto the set of some fictional drama and he had no idea who was who and what his lines were supposed to be. All he knew was that Tessa was pretty damn insistent that he hook up with Miss Marisa What's-her-name, irrespective of whether Gabe wanted the woman or not. The Realtor looked polished, confident, a Manhattan barracuda with teeth. Completely not his type. He liked his women…

Like Tessa.

That's what he wanted. Somebody that was soft and comfortable, that didn't care if they went out on Saturday night or stayed at home. Somebody that understood the rules of poker.

And, most of all, somebody that needed Gabe.

The way Tessa needed Gabe.

But, okay, she wanted to go down this pathway to disaster, then he'd walk down it, if only to show her how badly she was screwing up.

His smile was cruel.

Because Tessa was screwing up royally.

Marisa noticed Gabe looking in her direction and waved. Gabe motioned her over. A discreet dip of the head, nothing more and—zoom—she was at Gabe's bar.

Gabe took a deep breath and then proceeded to charm Miss Marisa Whoever right out of her senses. And he did. He complimented her dress, told her how the blue set off the twinkle in her eyes. He created a new drink, rum, vodka, and lemonade—and christened it the *Marisa,* insisting that everyone try it.

Tessa glowered at that one.

Inside, Gabe was beaming.

Everything was going along swimmingly until Daniel pulled him aside.

"What the hell are you doing?" asked his big brother, looking irate. This from a man whose general demeanor was somewhere between extracalm and not exactly breathing.

"What?"

"Why are you messing with this other girl? This can't be the woman you were talking to Sean about. Is it?"

"Sean told you?" snapped Gabe, glaring at his other brother and deciding he was going to kill Sean after all.

"Sean would tell the Pope if he got the chance. Why did you ever go to him for advice?"

"I didn't want to talk to you about it."

"Why?"

Gabe threw down his rag. "What is it with *why?* I don't want to tell you why, so I'm not going to. Deal with it, Daniel."

Daniel shifted his weight from one foot to the other. "Okay, look, I'm sorry for interfering, but you can't go messing up your life like this."

And now Daniel was drinking the same Kool-Aid as Tessa? "Messing up my life? What the— Daniel, I'm talking to a customer, that's it."

"No, you're doing the whole eye game with her, Gabe. It's like visual sex—and in front of everybody. Did you ever think you might be hurting somebody by doing that?"

"Hurting who?"

"Somebody," answered Daniel vaguely. Too vaguely.

"What are you talking about?"

"Why are you doing it?"

Gabe was tired of being accused of being a jerk for no good reason. It was about time he defended himself, because nobody else around here would, that was for damned sure. "Tessa wants me to go out with her. She's one of Tessa's friends. Some Realtor chick."

"Tessa?" Daniel stared over at Tessa, brows drawn together.

"Yes, Tessa. I'm doing her a favor," explained Gabe self-righteously. If there was anybody that deserved a medal, it was him.

"Why does Tessa want you to go out with somebody else?"

At that, Gabe threw up his arms. "How the hell should I know? Ask her. I'm going back to work. This is a bar, not the O.C., thank you very much. I'm going back to work. Going back to work now. And if you figure anything out, I don't want to know. I don't want to understand. I don't want to go boohoo. I just want to tend bar. *Capisce?*"

Daniel frowned but waved him away. "This is so wrong," he muttered, and Gabe was ready to throw a punch, but he'd never hit Daniel on purpose, and tonight wasn't the night to start. No, tonight he was going to pour drinks, flirt with the pretty lady and do exactly what Tessa wanted him to do.

Even if it hurt him.

TESSA WASN'T GOING TO watch. She wasn't going to watch. She wasn't going to watch. So then Lindy had to come by and tell her how Gabe was pulling a Sean with this new chick. And that it was completely weird because Gabe wasn't like Sean, and the woman was okay, but she wasn't that fabulous, but maybe she'd told him she could tongue him in the French-Bolivian way.

"What's the French-Bolivian way?"

"I made it up, Tessa. You know, guys get really jacked up

when you mention tongues. It's like verbal Viagra or something. Considering the mental hard-on he's got going over there, I'm thinking it has to be tongues."

Tessa didn't want to hear any more about tongues. "I'm going downstairs to smoke a cigarette."

Lindy looked at her, confused. "You don't smoke."

So why did everybody have to be so literal tonight? "I'm going to learn," she answered and then ran downstairs because she needed to get away, if only for a few minutes. Just long enough to pull herself together.

Once downstairs, she hid in the walk-in refrigerator, shivering in the cold, until a moment later when Daniel came in and sat next to her on a crate of limes. "You all right?" he asked as if it were completely normal to be sitting around in a refrigerator.

"Good. Of course, I'm good. No, I'm great," Tessa replied.

"You don't sound great."

"Does anybody really know how great sounds? We all have varying degrees of great, and I'm tipping the scales here."

He stayed silent for a minute, and she wondered why Daniel even cared about her well-being. He never was this sociable. Never. "Marisa is a friend of yours?" he asked.

"Yeah."

"She's a looker."

"And she's nice, too," said Tessa sweetly.

"That's why you're pushing her toward my brother?"

Tessa didn't like the way Daniel was looking at her. As though he knew things, things that she didn't want anybody to know. "She doesn't have cooties, if that's what you're trying to ask."

"Not asking. Merely trying to sort things out."

"Nothing to sort out," she said, forcing a laugh.

"You're sure?"

"Yeah. If you're thinking about the bet, don't worry. I'm

going to make Sean give everybody their money back. You won't lose." Technically Daniel should have won the first night. At one time, she would have insisted that he take the money, but now she didn't care. When she had a real job, she'd pay him the three thousand out of her own pocket.

"I'm worried about Gabe, not the bet, Tessa."

And, yes, he was worried about his brother, not the money. Wasn't that what families did? Protect each other? Tessa wanted to tell him that Gabe didn't need anybody worrying about him. He was unflappable, unsinkable, unassailable and every other *able* she could think of. *Able*. It was exactly the right word for Gabe. And Marisa. He and Marisa would get along fine. "Gabe's great," she muttered, crossing her arms across her chest, partially in defense and partially because the walk-in was freezing.

Daniel was unfazed. "I'll leave you alone."

"You do that, Daniel. Thanks."

8

GABE DIDN'T COME HOME on Saturday night and Tessa pretended not to notice. What did she expect? Instead she studied the real estate book and plucked her eyebrows for the first time in her life. And because she didn't want to face him when he did walk in the door, she changed for work and opted to spend Sunday afternoon in the park before heading to Prime.

Gabe wasn't scheduled to work that night, and Tessa was almost relieved.

Almost.

The truth was, she loved working with Gabe. Daniel was nice, but he didn't talk much. Sean was okay, but he didn't let anybody get too close. And Gabe was...well, Gabe was Gabe.

When she tossed a bottle his way, he caught it. When she juggled three lemons, he juggled four. When he started a joke, she knew the punch line.

God, she missed that.

When she got in, the Thursday afternoon irregulars were sitting at the bar.

"About time you showed up, missy. My glass has been empty for a full—" Charlie checked his old windup watch "—eight seconds."

"Why are you here on Sunday?"

"Lindy told me the yellow-sundress lady came here last Sunday. I want to find her. Wore my best tie."

Tessa smiled with relief. She'd rather be spending time

worrying about Charlie's love life than Gabe's. "You're looking spiffy, Charlie. I don't think that any woman could resist
you with those—" Tessa took a good look "—dollar signs and
Playboy logos running down your chest."

Charlie shrugged what had once been extrawide shoulders. "When you're my age, you don't need a tie for much."

Lloyd sniffed. "A man should always have appropriate attire."

Tessa slapped her rag in his general direction. "Charlie's
a free spirit."

EC nudged Charlie in the ribs. "That's her, isn't it?"

Sure enough, walking through the door were two young
ladies—way too young for Charlie. But his eyes lit up. "That's
her, but where's her grandmother?"

For a good ten minutes the men sat debating the wisdom
of whether Charlie should talk to the granddaughter or not,
and finally Tessa got miffed at all of them. No balls. Not a one.

Taking matters in hand, she approached the table where the
two girls were sitting. "Can I get you something?" she asked,
placing two bar napkins in front of them.

"Margarita on the rocks, no salt," said the first one.

"Appletini," said the second, and Tessa recognized her as
the girl who wore the yellow sundress, although today she was
in navy shorts and a classy tank top. "You've been in here
before, right?"

"Yeah, I work down the street."

"Weren't you here with an older woman?" Tessa looked at
the other girl. "No offense, of course, but I knew you were
way too young."

"That's my great-aunt. She's visiting from Kansas and
she swore that she remembered being in this place a long
time ago, but they called it something else. She made us
stop that day."

Tessa nodded, adopting her friendly tour-guide face.
"That's possible. Prime was O'Sullivan's a lot of years ago.

In fact, it was a speakeasy back during Prohibition. Your aunt has got a great memory. What's her name?"

"Irene Langford. I'm Kristine Langford."

Tessa leaned in low. "Listen, you see the group of old guys at the bar?" Kristine nodded. "One of them swears he knows your great-aunt. Maybe you could bring her in here sometime this week?"

"Really?" Kristine looked at the matched set of gray heads that were all turned in her direction. "That's so sweet. But she's not here anymore. She went back home."

Tessa tried to look perky for Charlie, but inside she felt something tear. When you got to be Charlie's age, opportunities were few and far between. "You expect her to visit again?"

"Doubt it. She's terrified of flying. The doctor had to slip her a Valium to get her on the plane in the first place. But can I tell her his name?"

Tessa thought for a minute, looked at Charlie's eager eyes, and nodded. "Charlie. Charlie Atwood."

"Charlie?"

"Uh-huh, the one in the tie—but don't hold it against him. I'll buy him another one," promised Tessa. "Let me get your drinks."

Tessa went back behind the bar and was immediately bombarded with eighty million questions.

"What's the woman's name?"

"Irene Langford."

"Langford? That doesn't sound right."

"Charlie, it's been a long time. I bet she's not who you think she is."

He frowned. "That's the problem. I can't remember who I think she is. I only remember the face. And there was a song."

"She's in Kansas now."

Charlie still didn't get it. "She'll be coming back?"

Tessa shook her head, hating to let the old guy down. He deserved better. "I don't think so."

Charlie stared into his mug until Lloyd tapped his glass to Charlie's. "To lost loves, lost nights and lost chances. But may you never lose your beer."

ON SUNDAY NIGHT GABE took out Marisa, just as Tessa wanted. He took her to 11 Madison for dinner and then some play that he didn't really understand, but she'd been all fired up to go, and, fine, Gabe wasn't up to disagreeing.

Marisa was nice enough, pretty enough, but man, the woman knew exactly what she wanted. When it came time to kiss her good-night or—God help him—something more serious, Gabe found himself dreading the whole ordeal.

This was one of the main reasons that he didn't date. Trying to understand what women expected, what they didn't expect, what they were saying, what they weren't saying. Did they expect to have sex on the first date? Would they think he was a creep if he wanted to have sex with them after one date? These were questions that could boggle and confuse a man's mind.

Still, he was going to do this. He was going to do this. Marisa looked up at him, smiled coyly, and he laid into her mouth.

Immediately she pulled back. "Okay, that was not good."

Under other circumstances, Gabe would have been insulted, but he liked Marisa's uncomfortable face because it proved that he'd been right and Tessa was wrong. And next time he saw her he was going to tell her that she shouldn't be fixing him up with other women—even if they were nice.

"Sorry," he said, noticing her confused expression. "My mind's elsewhere."

"Mine, too," she admitted. "You want to come up?" she asked.

"I should go home," he said, trying to figure out if "come up" was code for sex or not. And after that kiss there was no freaking way he was going near her for sex.

"I don't mean to *come up*," she said, adding suggestive emphasis. "I just thought you might want to talk for a few minutes."

Gabe checked his watch. It was too early to show up at the apartment with his pride still intact. A man didn't take getting dumped lightly, and who knew what Tessa's reasons were, but the fact was Tessa had dumped him.

Gabe nodded because a man needed his pride. "Sure."

They killed two hours discussing movies and arguing about whether chick flicks were a good thing or a bad thing. Marisa liked the Hamptons. Gabe liked the Jersey shore. Both agreed that subway fares were crazy expensive and the smoking ban in bars turned out to be all right after all.

They passed the time without incident when Gabe's cell rang, and he looked down to see his brother's cell number. He clicked the button. "Daniel?"

"Hello? Who's this?" asked a voice that wasn't Daniel's.

"This is Gabe. Who is this?" Gabe asked.

"This is Vincent, the bartender at Champs. Listen, I think your brother needs some help getting home. I tried to call a cab for him, but he wouldn't listen, and I'm not sure he knows where he's going."

"Daniel?" asked Gabe and then checked his watch. May twenty-fifth.

Damn.

While he'd been busy walking that tightwire that was Tessa, he'd forgotten about Daniel and Michelle's anniversary.

"Where's he at?" Gabe asked.

"We're in Westchester."

"Westchester? How'd he get up there?"

"Beats me. But he's been knocking back double scotches for the last three hours."

"He's alone?"

"Deep in his cups."

"I'm on my way."

Gabe hung up and looked at Marisa. "Sorry. I've got a brother to rescue."

"He's in Westchester?"

"Yeah. He's pretty smashed."

"You need a ride?" she asked, and he gave her high marks for seeing the problem right off.

"You have a car?"

"Of course," Marisa answered as if it was completely normal to keep a car in the city.

True, he didn't want to have sex with her, but she was thoughtful and capable. Tessa had good taste in friends. "Are you sure you don't mind? This won't be pretty."

"That's all right, I don't mind."

And they ended up on the FDR, cruising out onto the Deegan, until she wheeled onto the exit for Scarsdale.

Marisa had a sweet little convertible and a heavy accelerator foot, but Gabe was happy for the rush. Daniel didn't do this often, but when he did, Gabe was always there to bail him out.

The sports bar was on the main street in Scarsdale, a place with six TVs, flashing neon beer signs and bartenders dressed in striped referee uniforms that no man in his right mind would ever wear in a drinking establishment.

Hunched over said bar, blindingly drunk, was the O'Sullivan brother formerly known as "the sensible one."

Gabe rushed forward. "Daniel?"

The bartender looked up in relief. "It was either you or the cops."

"Does he come in here often?" asked Gabe.

"Never seen him before, but I've only been working here for a few weeks."

Gabe paid the tab and gave the bartender a substantial tip. "Sorry."

"He's your brother?"

"Yeah."

"Kept talking about some woman."

"Michelle?"

"No, he kept talking about Anastasia."

Anastasia? Gabe shook his head, deciding the bartender was confused. "Doesn't matter."

He looked over at Marisa, who was watching the scene with interest. "You sure you want to do this?"

"It's the most excitement I've had since a famous Grammy winner walked into the office, and I got to show him a SoHo loft that would have paid my rent for a year."

With a quick smile, she took a shoulder, Gabe took the other one, and they carried Daniel toward the door.

"He doesn't usually do this," Gabe said, needing to defend Daniel.

"I'm not one to judge."

"He lost his wife on 9/11," he told her, not wanting to say too much, but he didn't want Marisa thinking his brother was a lush, but Daniel kept things bottled inside, and when they came out, it was never pretty—and usually incoherent.

"Oh, I'm sorry. Where are we headed?"

"He's got a place down in Battery Park." He searched Daniel's pocket for keys and found them—thank God—because he wasn't up to explaining this to Tessa. Trying to explain it to the absolute stranger that was Marisa was bad enough.

It took some work, but they got him in the backseat, and Gabe climbed in next to him.

"He's kind of sad."

"Not sad," muttered Daniel.

The car shot forward, and soon Gabe was sitting there in a strange woman's car with a drunk brother who looked as if was going to wake up tomorrow and hopefully forget all of this. Gabe wasn't up to reminding him, or correcting him, but he could feel Marisa's curiosity in the darkness.

Finally Gabe broke the silence. "I don't know what to do. I don't know how to talk to him. I don't know what to say. I don't know what not to say. I want to pretend like nothing ever happened, but that's wrong, too."

"Has he been to counseling?"

"Daniel? Uh, no."

"Why not?" she asked calmly.

"He's not the counseling type," Gabe responded, because nobody in their right mind went to counseling, and the O'Sullivans were all in their right minds, at least most of the time.

"Oh," she said, then went back to being quiet.

Gabe glanced at Daniel, noted the nodding head, and sighed. One of the most frustrating things was that Gabe could usually fix anything—personal problem, leaky faucet, clogged beer tap. But lately he was striking out left and right. First with Tessa, now with Daniel. For a man who prided himself on the ability to handle every problem thrown his way, this wasn't good. "You think I should do something, don't you? Take him to a shrink or read some books to figure out how to talk to my own brother." Yeah, he sounded defensive. So what?

"I don't know."

They didn't say anything more on the way to the building, but Gabe knew that Marisa didn't approve of Gabe. Easy for her to make judgments when there was no right or wrong, no good or bad, just a man who had a hole where his heart used to be.

It wasn't right.

Daniel's building was down near Wall Street, within the shadow of where the towers had stood.

Marisa eased the car into a parking garage and Gabe looked at her in surprise. "You can drop us off. I can take it from here."

Marisa claimed the ticket from the attendant and shrugged. "You might need some help, and it's not like I have somewhere to be."

Gabe gave her a long look and then waved it off. "Your choice."

Daniel was incoherent in the back, so Gabe was grateful for the help, and they lugged Daniel upstairs to his apartment.

When they entered the apartment, Marisa looked around. "Nice place. One bedroom but roomy. And the view's good."

Gabe smiled, maneuvering Daniel out of his suit jacket. He was the only man Gabe knew who would get shit-faced in a jacket and tie. "You sound like Tessa. No wonder you two are friends."

"She's nice," Marisa offered and then ran forward when Daniel started to tilt.

"Just remember to stay on her good side." Gabe smiled slightly.

"I don't think she has a bad side."

"You don't know her well enough."

"You two are roommates?"

Gabe wheeled Daniel toward the bedroom. "It's a temporary thing. She needed a place to live. I had space."

"That's kind of you."

"She would do the same for me."

"Yeah. Yeah, I think she would."

With one finger pressed to his brother's chest, he landed Daniel on the bed. Daniel was going to be out for a long, long time. Gabe looked at the clock, saw that it was three, and suppressed a yawn.

"You don't have to sit up. I'll take the first watch. I think your brother's out for a few hours." Marisa was fast becoming a saint in Gabe's eyes.

"You don't mind?"

"Nah. I'll turn the television on."

Gabe gave her a hard look. "I'm sorry about earlier. Too bad it didn't work. I like you."

Marisa looked at Daniel, looked at Gabe and then shrugged. "Maybe it wasn't meant to be."

GABE STAGGERED HOME ON Monday morning. Tessa hadn't wanted to stay up, but she had. But when she heard the key in the lock, she dashed back to her room and pretended to be asleep. Not for long, though, because eventually her masochistic tendencies got the better of her. Tessa had to know.

She came out, rubbing her head, hoping he wouldn't notice the coffeepot that was filled with fresh coffee.

Sadly Gabe didn't look as if he was noticing much. His eyes were red, and his wrinkled shirt looked as if it had been pulled from the clothes hamper.

"How was the date?" asked Tessa, keeping her face casually interested, not wanting to read too much into appearances—telling as they were.

"Great," answered Gabe.

"Great is good," she said and then pulled out her box of cereal. "Wa some?" she ased, holding out a handful—which, af he declined, she forced herself to eat. The cereal tasted like cardboard or that plastic food that restaurants kept out on display for decades at a time. Neither of which Tessa had an appetite for.

Gabe watched her for a minute and then shook his head. "I'm tired. I'm going to bed."

"You going to see her again?" asked Tessa as she watched him walk down the hall. He looked so tired, so exhausted, and she knew exactly why he was so tired, and the rock in her gut knew exactly why he was so tired, too.

Then Gabe turned around, spearing her with a glance. "Do you want me to see her again?"

With those bloodshot eyes and a shirt that should have

been burned, Tessa knew she had to tread carefully. "Do you like her?" she asked, which seemed noncommittal enough. If he said yes, then she'd know that her fling with Gabe had been nothing more than that. A fling.

"She's nice enough," he answered, completely noncommittal—but not a yes, either.

"Yeah," agreed Tessa.

Gabe rubbed his eyes. "Yeah, she's nice or, yeah, you want me to go out with her again?"

"Yeah, she's nice."

He squinted at her. "Did you change your eyebrows?"

Self-consciously she smoothed them back. "It's called grooming."

He nodded once. "It looks nice." Then he stared at the door to his bedroom, then stared back at Tessa. Then he sighed. "Are you ever going to tell me why I'm jumping through all these hoops, Tessa?"

There was something so disarming about the look in those blue eyes. This was the man who probably knew her better than anyone in New York.

She owed him something; she owed him the truth. "Because you scare me," she said, the words coming out in a rush.

The bloodshot eyes looked at her, confused, as though it wasn't the answer he'd expected. "Why? I'm the most unscary person on the planet."

And for Tessa, that exact unscariness was the reason he was so dangerous to her well-being. If he was as raunchy as Sean, or as serious as Daniel, she'd have her shields up, and it'd be easy to keep a relationship alive while chasing her career. But Gabe wasn't like most men. Her shields had never even had a chance.

"I need time, Gabe. That's all. I have things I have to do first. I have to learn to be on my own."

"I'm tired of your rules, I'm tired of your guidelines. Damn, right now I'm tired."

He did look tired, and she hated that she was doing this, but if she didn't do it now, she never would. He didn't know how weak she really was. She had to make sure she could make it on her own. She had to make sure with one hundred percent certainty that if she needed to support herself, she could. Nobody seemed to understand that but her.

She stared into his tired eyes and willed herself to be strong. "I've known you for four years. You're the first person I met in New York. The first person who offered me a job, the first person who made sure I understood the difference between a local and an express train, the first person who explained to me how to cross against the light in order to not be run over by the eight thousand people crossing against the light from the opposite direction. There's no one that I've ever depended on more, Gabe. Nobody. Not even Denny. I can't depend on you like that."

Gabe, who had taken care of himself for his entire life, shrugged easily. "Yes, you can."

"I have to learn to depend on myself first."

"Tessa you can do anything you want." He ran a hand through his hair. Dark, silky hair that probably Marisa had touched the way Tessa longed to.

Now wasn't the time to think about his hair, she reminded herself. "You're right. I can do anything I want. But I have to actually *do* it. I can't just *want* to do it. There's a difference."

He took that in, and she could see the wheels turning in his head. Finally he nodded. "How long are we talking about here? A month? Another four years?"

And now they were discussing schedules. Tessa, who was about five years off hers, felt the familiar panic rise up inside her. "I don't know."

Gabe frowned, not sensing her panic, probably because he never panicked. Never felt that urgency at three in the morning, when she stared up at the ceiling, thinking of what she should be doing with her life and how much of a failure she would be if she didn't decide soon.

"Do you know where I was last night?" he asked.

"Yeah," answered Tessa, not really wanting to have this conversation.

"No. No, you don't. It was Daniel's wedding anniversary last night. Do you know how many wedding anniversaries he and Michelle had?"

"No," she said, not understanding what Daniel's wife had to do with his date with Marisa.

"Not a single one. They were married exactly five months before she was killed and never had one anniversary. Do you know what my brother did last night, Tessa?"

"No."

"He got drunk. Falling down drunk in some bar in West-chester that I don't even know how he ended up at. Sometimes it's their anniversary, sometimes it's her birthday and some-times it's nothing at all. My brother had a total of ten months with Michelle, and that was it. All my life I've been sur-rounded by people whose time was up before it was supposed to be, and nobody knows what'll happen. We could all go tomorrow and—poof—we never would have had a chance. So you can see why I'm not eager to sit on my hands while you move forward with your life. I don't want to end up drunk in a sports bar in Westchester because you needed time."

"I'm sorry," answered Tessa. And she was. She hated that people had to hurt. She hated that Daniel was hurt—he didn't deserve that. She hated that Gabe was hurt—he didn't deserve it either. But Tessa couldn't fix the problems of the world, she had to focus on fixing Tessa. She had to fix herself or she never would. And maybe it didn't matter to Gabe, maybe it didn't matter to Daniel, maybe it didn't matter to anyone but Tessa, but this was her last shot and she knew it. There were other people who could start over at thirty or start over at forty, or start over at sixty-five, but Tessa had never started at all. At some point she had to get out of the gate, and the clock was ticking.

"It doesn't matter to me if you're who you want to be or who you are, Tessa. You're you. That's enough for me. Why don't we go slow? You want to do your class. Stay here."

"I don't know that I can do that, Gabe," she said, even though she knew she couldn't. Gabe was a long stretch of pristine beach looking out over the ocean. The summer breeze blowing across your skin, warming you, making you drowsy and relaxed. Tessa remembered those long, lazy days by the water, hours passing as you did nothing but lay there catching rays.

He met her eyes. "Don't make me wait too long, because patience is too close to failure for me."

"I won't," she said, feeling the panic moving up her throat. Panic that tasted remarkably like cold cereal.

Tessa swallowed it down. Keeping away from Gabe was the hardest thing she'd ever done, but she knew she didn't have a choice, and maybe tomorrow she'd feel as if she'd conquered the world, but right now she felt like garbage.

So she smiled at him as if she'd just conquered the world. "Starts on Wednesday. Eight o'clock to five o'clock for ten straight days. I needed to talk to you about my schedule. I can't be there until after five, when class is over. And then when I get my license, I think I should put in my two weeks notice at the bar. I'm going to make this work."

"Sure," he said, then gave her one last disappointed look. Their eyes locked, and she longed to take the easy way out, to run to him and ditch every damned goal she'd ever set for herself. It was just like before, when she was young and naive. However, this time she was older, wiser—and this time she was close to achieving what she wanted. So close. If he'd only give her the time to succeed. That was all she wanted. Time. And Gabe.

She sighed, a long, slow exhale of air because she needed to remember to breathe.

His gaze did move off her. Onto something new. "I'm going to bed."

ON TUESDAY, TESSA HAD to turn in her application and fees for the real-estate class. As she got ready to leave, she messed with her hair for two hours in the bathroom. But even after two hours it still didn't look any better. She pulled it back, she moussed it (that'd been a mistake), she wore a headband and then finally she combed it back down into her eyes, just the way she always wore it. But still she wasn't satisfied. The thing about making over your life was that you wanted to do it in strappy heels and head-turning lipstick—and without a man's name tattooed on your butt.

A trip to Sephora killed two nights' worth of tips, but in exchange, she was now in possession of the handiwork of the devil.

Makeup.

Mascara, concealer, an eyelash curler, pressed powder, lip gloss, eye shadow, liner, foundation and four high-dollar tubes of lipstick. Tessa lined them up in a neat little row and studied them all carefully, taking note of what she was about to do.

Today she was moving one necessary step closer to the dark side, using tools designed to make women more appealing to men. Makeup was worn by women who lived with men, women who needed men to support them, women who needed male approval in order to feel fulfilled as a woman.

Women like Marisa.

Marisa, who was going to get her into Hudson Towers. There, Tessa felt her sense of resolve return.

Hudson Towers. A place to go home to after a hard day's work, with no worries about tomorrow. She could look at the New York skyline and know that she had conquered them all.

That was power.

That was success.

Tessa smiled as though she were happy.

After utilizing the handiwork of the devil, she stared at herself in the mirror and decided that, yes, that devil was one smart dude. She looked awesome. Except for the hairstyle—or lack thereof.

Tomorrow she would get her tattoo removed. But then she pulled at the waist of her jeans, looked at the scarlet letters and decided that, no, she was going to keep it until she passed her real-estate exam. After that, the tattoo was gone. History. And her transformation would be complete.

As she went on the subway, she noticed the looks in men's eyes, the envy from women, too. She turned in her application, paid the fees in cash, and said thank you to the lady at the desk as if she had the world at her feet.

The woman was polite and smiled, until the next lady showed up behind Tessa with strappy heels, head-turning lipstick and a killer hairstyle.

Tessa knew she didn't have a choice. She was going to make over her life, her face, her feet and, yes, her hair. After that, she could have dessert. Namely on Gabe O'Sullivan à la mode.

She sped into a salon that she normally couldn't afford, but this was for her career. She was changing her life, and the usual discount place wasn't going to cut it anymore.

By the time she left, Francois had turned her into a veritable swan. And, sadly, because she needed to show it off, and Marisa wouldn't understand, and her family was in Florida, she had no place to go but Prime.

Tessa hesitated outside the place, feeling nervous and foolish, but so what? She needed someone to tell her she looked good. She needed Gabe to tell her she looked good.

She pulled open the heavy door and walked in as if she owned the joint, which she didn't.

Sean whistled and Charlie adjusted his glasses.

Gabe smiled.

Not wanting to tempt fate, she sat in front of Sean.

"I could have sex with you," he said. "I just need to get that out in the open. Not that I want you to think I'm a shallow SOB whose head gets turned by a long neck and a great ass, but I can't help who I am, and I believe in being honest and up front with women. So they know exactly what they're getting. Besides a good time, I mean."

"Thank you," Tessa said primly.

It took thirty-three minutes for Gabe to approach her. She kept track. "You look good," he said when Sean went off to get a phone number from some woman nearby.

"Thank you," she said, basking in his warmth for only a little bit. She had always loved the beach.

"Ready for class?"

"I've been studying."

"You don't need to study for this. You can do apartment rentals and sales in your sleep."

"Maybe. But the class isn't about which buildings allow pets. I have to know contracts and finance and insurance and equal-opportunity laws."

"You'll still do fine. Any luck with the roommate situation? The phone's been quiet."

"I think I found a place. Should come open in about three weeks."

"Really?"

"And I'll be living single," she said proudly.

"Very nice," he said, but he didn't look happy.

"Yeah. Finally. It's only been twenty-six years."

"You've got a lot to celebrate."

"Yes, yes, I do. For the first time in my life I have something to celebrate. I'm going to head out now. Test out my new look on somebody else besides these losers."

"That's a good idea. Head over to the Carlyle. Classy place. Elegant. Like you."

"I think I will. I've never been in there before."

She could feel him watching her as she walked out the door.

Tessa smiled. Maybe it would be okay after all.

GABE LEFT SEAN IN CHARGE of closing, which was normally a recipe for disaster, but tonight he didn't care. Tessa needed him and he knew it. She wasn't a woman to go sit in bars alone like Marisa. She'd start talking to some used-car salesman from Omaha who was away from his wife for the first time in twenty years. And he'd want to get laid and he'd monopolize Tessa's time for four hours until it was last call, and then she'd feel bad, but tell the guy no, and he would get all pissed off at her and yell, and Tessa didn't need that kind of crap.

So Gabe took a quick shower, pulled out the black pants and shirt that he kept in the back of his closet for special nights and headed for the Carlyle.

He saw her immediately, sitting at the bar, a middle-aged toupee type sitting three seats away, giving her the eye.

Gabe sighed. When he was right, he was right.

He leaned against the wall, content to watch her for a while. There were women who took your breath away, and then there were women who were pure oxygen. That was Tessa.

Another lowlife hit on her, and she smiled politely, buying the loser a drink only because she felt sorry. Another lowlife came up, a little more forceful than the last, and her perfectly shaped brows curved downward, signaling a woman in need of rescuing.

Cue Gabe.

"Hi," he said, taking the seat next to her.

Tessa looked up, her eyes startled, and she began to say something—probably *no,* but he wasn't going to give her a chance. Gabe put a finger on her mouth. Tonight they'd do things her way. "No. We've never met."

For a second she looked at him the way he'd dreamed she would look at him. Her green eyes were soft and filled with things that a used-car salesman from Omaha would never understand. Yes, there were definite advantages to doing things her way.

"Why are you drinking alone? A beautiful woman like you? You should have dozens of men buying you drinks, but instead you're buying them all drinks. If you worked in a bar, you'd know this. That's not the way it's supposed to be."

"If wishes were horses…"

"Can I get you something to drink, Miss I-Can't-Follow-the-Rules? Maybe some champagne? Or a cosmopolitan. You're looking very cosmopolitan tonight."

She shook her head. "No champagne. Diet soda, I think."

"You must be a lightweight."

"No, champagne sounds flat."

"I'm sorry," he said, wishing it were perfect. She should have perfect.

"Don't be."

"What are you celebrating?"

She tried to smile at him. "Being alone."

"Bad breakup?"

"It hurt."

Gabe told himself to be careful. With the look in her eyes, the tight curve of her lips, he could easily forget about taking things slow. But this one answer he had to know. "Any regrets?"

"Nah," she said, slaying him with a single word. "It had to be done."

"You want me to leave?"

Her gaze scanned his face, up and down, back and forth, as if he were a piece of art and not a living, breathing man— although he was currently not breathing.

Tessa licked her lips slowly, carefully, and he still didn't breathe. "It makes me a weak person if I don't want you to leave, and I don't want to be weak, but I don't want you to leave, either."

Gabe took a breath. "I don't think you're weak."

"I do," she said, sounding so sad, so lonely, and he hated that wanting to be with him made her sad. It shouldn't happen that way. He shouldn't want to take advantage of it, but, goddamn, he couldn't stop. How could he stop?

Silently Gabe got up, refusing to look at the heartbreak in her eyes. Tessa looked at him, startled, but didn't keep him.

They'd both be better off if he left.

TESSA KNEW GABE HAD done the right thing. He was trying to give her the time she'd asked for. She waved over the bartender.

"I'll take a tequila shot," she ordered, which was her panacea for most everything in the world.

She looked around the bar, seeing the cartoons on the wall, the beautiful people who were laughing and living here.

She didn't belong.

When Gabe sat next to her, she could pretend, and it was fun to pretend, but it was nothing more than pretend.

She rubbed a finger around the rim of the glass, tasting the tang of alcohol, and then Gabe returned.

He ordered a beer and didn't say a word to her, but there was a key in front of him. Not a car key, not a key to the bar, not a key to all her problems, but a hotel room key.

He stayed silent, wouldn't even look at her. She was about to walk away, about to practice her newfound strength and courage, but then she noticed the number etched on the metal.

Ten twenty-three.

Her birthday.

Oh, he didn't fight fair. Of course, he hadn't fought fair since the moment he'd walked through the door.

He still didn't look at her, but she heard his words, so quietly, so thoroughly irresistible. "I'm heading upstairs. Your choice."

THE ROOM WAS DARK when she entered except for the night lights of the city burning through the open drapes. But the lights weren't dim enough to hide behind. Tessa couldn't pretend anymore. She couldn't act as if he was some stranger, some fantasy that she'd created.

Gabe stood next to the window, looking out, not looking at her. "I wasn't sure you'd show," he said.

Tessa came to stand beside him, concentrating on the Manhattan skyline, trying to ignore the quiet sound of his breathing, the crisp aroma of his cologne. But she couldn't ignore it, any more than she could ignore him.

It didn't matter if all her senses were dead, she would recognize him, feel the warmth that shone through him. He was her sun, luring her closer. "I wasn't sure I'd show either," she answered, because tonight wasn't a night for secrets. She'd kept too many things from him, too many things from herself, but for once she didn't want to pretend, didn't want to keep any more secrets.

"I'm glad you came."

"Gabe..." she started and finally he turned. Finally he looked at her, and nothing had ever scared her more than the bold determination in his eyes. She'd thought he was playing her games, but somewhere the rules had changed, and now the rules were all his...and she felt a surge of relief that surprised her.

"Sssh... No names. No worries. Nothing but you and me. Nobody else."

Tessa came to him then the way she had always wanted to do, kissing him the way she'd always yearned to do, kissing him as if they were together. She loved his mouth, loved the way he kissed her, so desperately, so feverishly, like he was going to die if he didn't touch her. Because she felt that way. That same hot fever burned in her blood. And being here, in an anonymous hotel room with Manhattan on the other side of a glass pane, seemed the perfect place to make love to a man she didn't want to love. Here, she didn't have to worry about tomorrow. She would wake up at three in the morning, and he would be lying beside her in bed. And after that? No, that she wouldn't think about. Not tonight.

Her arms curled around him, wrapping around his neck, clinging in the way she'd always desired but hadn't dared.

One of his arms curved behind her back, keeping her locked to him, and she loved being so close to him, loved the feel of his heart underneath her breast, loved the feel of his arousal between her legs. And then his hand was at her blouse, working the buttons, and his fingers were shaking.

Gabe, with the steadiest hands in New York, was shaking.

He peeled the silk back from her torso, pressing long, heated kisses against her skin. First her arms, her neck, then her shoulders. As if he'd never seen shoulders before in his life.

"You have beautiful shoulders," he whispered, his mouth pressing against her. "The perfect curve." Tessa wanted to argue, to tell him shoulders were too bony to be beautiful, but she couldn't talk, she only wanted to listen. She wanted to listen to this forever.

Her fingers worked at the buttons on his shirt, removing it, then skimming to find the heated flesh that was underneath. Her hands searched, explored, tracing the soft whorls of hair on his chest, testing the heavy band of muscles that lay over his stomach, circling the bulk of his arm. She explored him as if he belonged to her. "I've always wanted to do this," she confessed.

Then he cupped her breasts in his palms, and she ached to cover herself because she wasn't big in the chest—32A only made it so far—but his fingers were so careful, so cautious, as if she were made of spun glass. Tenderly he traced the outline of her nipple, and in the dim light she could see the concentration on his face, the intensity in the hard line of his jaw.

It was like seeing another man. Someone she'd never met before. Someone who made her feel so outrageously beautiful. *Gabe.*

His fingers worked the zipper on her skirt, touching her here and there, everywhere, turning her into liquid fire, and she could feel the cool air as the material slid down her legs, leaving her clad only in stockings, panties and one brand-new pair of strappy heels.

She heard the hiss of his breath as he looked at her, and she felt his fingers glide along her leg, gliding over the silk of her stockings, her body following the slow play of his hand.

Her thighs pressed together, one moment hiding her from him, the next opening before him. He cursed softly, reverently, and she smiled because she'd heard him swear so many times before but never again would it sound the same. She would always remember this one timeless moment.

His mouth took hers then, tasting her, and she matched him, her tongue dancing in his mouth. Slowly he walked her toward the bed, laying her back, her bare skin against the soft down. The intoxicating smell of him was a powerful aphrodisiac.

A hard body pressed her into the mattress, and she smiled. They'd never made love in a bed before. It seemed so completely mundane to be here, so completely perfect. He rolled her on top of him, kissing her mouth, his chest pressing into her breasts, the hard erection between his legs moving against her.

Tessa worked the fly of his pants, pushing them down on his legs, touching the crisp hair there, marveling at the power of his thighs bunching beneath her touch.

Her mouth explored the muscles at his waist, feeling them dance when her lips caressed his skin. She took away the briefs, her hand cupping him. For the first time she dared to trace the long vein that ran underneath his skin. Tessa could feel the heated blood, watched the dark flush on his face that accompanied each touch of her hand.

This—this—was power. She could feel it singing inside her. Her muscles flexed, her senses took over.

She touched him with her mouth. Heard his groan, and she smiled to herself. She tasted and sucked and used her tongue in the French-Bolivian way, and it didn't matter if there wasn't a French-Bolivian way, because now there was. In her own mind, there was nothing more sensual, nothing more exotic nothing more decadent than being here with Gabe.

His big body jerked beneath her mouth, and when she heard him swear in frustration, Tessa's smile turned into a grin. Gabe, who never missed a step, never dropped a glass was currently at her mercy, and she'd never been so turned on in her life.

She looked at him, wiggled her eyebrows and heard him groan. And then she got serious. Mr. Gabriel Cormac Sila O'Sullivan was out of control, fabulously out of control, and all because of little Tessa Hart.

Her hands mapped the long line of his leg, the strong curve of his butt, the heavy sacks underneath his sex and the ridge of muscles that lined his stomach. Sweat covered his skin with a glistening sheen as she tormented him, alternately teasing then delighting him as her mouth moved up and down over his shaft. He smelled marvelously alive, a mix of citrus cologne, soap and him. Mixed into it was the scent of her. She could smell it on him. Everywhere she touched, her perfume lingered, the musk of her desire staying behind, blending with his, bonding them together.

His cursing grew more severe, more erratic, and his head fell back against the pillows. With the Manhattan skyline in view, she could see the heavy beat of his pounding heart. Under her hand, she could feel the pulse of his blood.

He swore again, his sex jumping, and she thought he was

going to come, just as she wanted him to. She thought that she'd done this to him. But she was wrong.

Gabe twisted her underneath him, parted her legs, his head rearing back. In one sharp thrust he was inside her, and Tessa felt her body seize, frozen in place.

"You do this to me," he breathed and then he began to move, pounding there, stroke after stroke. Her legs locked around him; she matched him with each surge of his hips, felt the pleasure rise inside her, threatening to overtake her.

The orgasm came like an afternoon storm, raging in its intensity, and Tessa felt him pour inside of her. Her body went lax, and she lay there, bundled in strong arms, sheltered from the rest of the world. Two souls together alone. She pressed a soft kiss against his bare shoulder, tasting the skin, tasting the sweat, and she smiled.

Gabe took her chin in his hand and made her look at him, not letting her turn away, not letting her run. Tonight she didn't want to run, not anymore. It was hard staring at him, because she knew there were things in her eyes that she didn't want him to see. Not yet. Not while her life was still in flux. But she let him see because there was something in his blue eyes that matched her heart. *Maybe, maybe,* she thought.

"I love you," he whispered, and the words cut into her skin, into her mind, into her heart. She'd known this. Deep down, she'd known those words, known they'd existed, known they were out there, drifting high in the air, just above the noise of the city, the shouts of the bar, the endless clamor of her life. They were there, just waiting for her to pull them close, and this time, in the quiet darkness, she did.

Words tripped on her tongue because Tessa wasn't sure or confident. Her life was a mess, and on a scale of one to ten, her consistency factor was a minus seven, but the best thing in her life, the one constant, the one fixture, the one steady state was Gabe.

So she kissed him, long, slow, deep, but not because of his support or his comfort. This wasn't about career aspirations or power. This was something deeper, something infinitely more precious.

Tessa knew.

Somehow in the last four years, sometime between the first time he'd said hello and the last time he'd moved her soul, somewhere, somehow, she couldn't deny the truth anymore.

Tessa was in love.

GABE WOKE WITH THE sun in his eyes and a smile on his lips. Life did not get sweeter than this. Tessa was perfect in his arms, and he wished he had thought of the whole hotel thing sooner. Sometimes a person just needed a good kick in the butt in order to see things correctly, and this was just the kick in the butt that Tessa needed. And what a nice butt it was, too, he thought, sliding a hand over the smooth skin.

And a tattoo.

It was the first time he'd noticed it there, the first time he'd seen her nude in the daylight. And seeing another man's name branded on flesh that belonged to him didn't sit right in Gabe's universe.

Eventually the red fog cleared from his vision and his normal demeanor returned. A tattoo. So what? Besides, there were ways to get tattoos removed. They weren't permanent—or completely permanent. Right then she turned, blinked once, and then smiled up at him, and he felt his heart turn over. This was home, right here with her beside him.

"Good morning, Tessa," he said, his voice still husky with sleep, but his body was feeling pretty damned awake, thank you very much. He dipped his head to taste her mouth and then lingered there.

Soon her mouth wasn't enough, and he lingered on her breast, as well. She whacked him on the shoulder, and he raised his head, insulted that she would dare interrupt such a heartfelt tribute to the perfect human body that just happened to be hers.

"What?" he asked, surprised to see that she was blushing.

"I should get dressed," she answered, and he heard the tone. It was back. Gabe really hated that tone—and he had thought that after last night the tone would have disappeared forever.

Hello, tone.

Still, he was a fast learner. His hand slipped lower, slipping inside her, finding her warm and wet. Did the tone really matter that much?

"It's early," he said and then checked the clock just to make sure he was right. "It's not even six."

"I start class today."

Man. There were very few things that could deflate Gabe's current energetic state. To be honest, real-estate class was the one.

"You're killing the mood, Tessa."

"Sorry," she said, not meeting his eyes. Another danger sign. Okay, he could deal. Things were good. She was good. He was good. Best of all, they were good. What was a little eye avoidance?

"I can take a hint," he muttered with an exaggerated sigh. Light, easy. Not a problem here. Then Gabe slid out of bed and walked over to the windows, amazed by the view. There was something very exhilarating about New York in the morning. It was better than coffee, much better. He took a deep, long breath, clearing his lungs.

Hell, yeah. New opportunities, new life, new hope. This was his kind of town.

Gabe turned, watched Tessa, still rumpled in the covers, and smiled. Definitely his kind of town. "I'm going in the shower, and you should know that I have ablutophobia—a terrifying fear of showers. I bet you didn't realize that."

She smiled at him, the sun beaming on her face. "I did not know that."

"If you were a friend, you wouldn't abandon me to my fears."

Her gaze slid down and, yeah…so he got a little harder? If she got an eyeful, she had only herself to blame. "I shouldn't."

"As a bartender, I hear that a lot."

Then she slid out of bed, sleek legs emerging, and his smile faded. Good God, she was beautiful. Somehow he had never really noticed that before. The sun hit her for only a second, touching her skin in ways that made him stupidly jealous. Her breasts were small but pert, with nipples that were the color of Kahlúa and could knock you flat-ass on the floor just as easily.

And the new hair? That was growing on him, too. It was a lot more sophisticated than the simple job she had before. Although, at first the cut seemed wrong for Tessa…until you noticed the way her shoulders sloped so perfectly from her neck.

Shoulders?

Yes, he was losing it.

When she headed for the bathroom, he watched her walk, watched the sway in her hips, and right before his eyes, she switched, presto change-o. Now you see Tessa the bartender. Now you don't. In her place was a teasing sylph that he couldn't keep his eyes off.

Stupidly, he followed.

THE SHOWER WAS BOTH HIS punishment for her and his reward, as well. The Carlyle spared no expense in bathrooms, and a man could do much damage to a woman's mental health with a potent force of water and a heavy dose of tongue.

Gabe toweled off his hair, watching as she searched for her clothes. He could get used to this casual-domesticity stuff. He'd never lived with a woman before, never had the desire to, but he also knew that life with Tessa was something that he didn't want to live without. Tessa was obsessed with tomorrow, but Gabe lived only for today, and today was perfect.

Something had changed between them last night. He'd used the L word; she hadn't run. In fact, he'd bet his bar that she loved him back. He wasn't sure how it happened, or when it happened but somehow it did, and he was going to keep her. Probably forever.

Now he just had to figure out how to broach this without scaring her. And forget about the new place. Tessa belonged with him—he only had to convince her. "You found a new apartment?"

Tessa stopped her search, her blouse disappointingly wadded against her chest. "Yeah."

It was probably some rat trap with a sleazeball of a landlord and seven stories of stairs to climb every day. His place was so much nicer than anything she could come up with on her own. In fact, he'd let her keep her own room. She'd probably like that piece of independence. But she'd have to get a bigger bed.

"Where?" he asked curiously.

"Hudson Towers," she answered.

Gabe kept his smile fixed in place because he wasn't one to jump to conclusions or make snap judgments or get jacked up about things that on the surface might seem out of whack. He prided himself on that. "Amazing."

"It came out of the blue," she said, pulling on her skirt, still not meeting his eyes.

Gabe watched her dress, waiting for her to add to this conversation, but Tessa wasn't adding one single detail. What a freaking miracle.

"Marisa?" he prodded, still smiling.

She nodded and he saw her swallow. Saw that telltale bump in her throat, saw the panic in the green eyes.

He kept smiling, and Gabe was pretty damned proud of himself for that. "She's a good friend. I can see why you wanted me to go out with her. Is there anything you want to tell me?" he asked, because he was absolutely one hundred percent certain that this was nothing more than a misunderstanding. That Tessa would never sell him out for an apartment. Because that wasn't who she was. Tessa wouldn't sell out the devil.

"Nope, nothing to say." And all thoughts of casual domesticity blew out the window.

"You're going to take it, aren't you?" he asked, already knowing the answer. Of course she was going to take it. This was Tessa. This was *Hudson Towers,* the world's most perfect apartment building. In the big scheme of things, Gabe couldn't compete with real estate.

Nope. Not with Tessa.

Right then he didn't feel like talking, really didn't feel like being there.

He pulled on the rest of his clothes, not bothering to look up.

"Don't go," she asked, her voice wavering, but when he looked at her this time, he saw the new and improved haircut, the new and improved shoes, the new and improved steel in her eyes.

And last night all but disappeared. Forever slid down the drain. And Gabe was left with his heart on a platter right out there for her to eat? No, that one still stuck in the gut.

His eyes met hers. His face plastered with that same smile. "Three weeks before you move? We can get you packed up in three weeks. You'll need to think about your deposits for the utilities and then you need to check on the rental application—"

"I can handle it," she said, interrupting him before he could educate her on the ins and outs of having an apartment in your own name. "Gabe, we can still be together."

And suddenly he couldn't keep up the easygoing Gabe charade. Not anymore. "Oh? Was that part of the deal? You can still sleep with me, too?"

"That wasn't it."

"What was *it*, Tessa?"

She waited, hesitated, trying to spin this into something noble. But Tessa didn't have Gabe's gift with words. No, Tessa always shot straight and true. And she did it again, even if it was going to cost her. "If I got you to go out with her, she'd get me in the building."

She drew her lips together, and now there was steel there, too. Damn, little Tessa Hart was turning into one cold princess.

"Wow. I guess every girl has her price."

Her eyes flashed, the man showing a small chink. "I had a chance. I took it. It's not a price. It's an apartment, a living space, four walls and a ceiling."

"It's a thing, Tessa. It doesn't have feelings, it doesn't have emotions. It can't get hurt, like people can. It's a thing, nothing more."

"Maybe to you, but I need to be alone, I need to live on my own. I need to know that I can do this. Because at one time, when I had to make a choice between a man and a career, I chose the man, and all I ended up with was his name tattooed on my ass. No career, no means to take care of me, I was just thrown out there without a lifeboat. I wanted to be able to take care of myself, but I couldn't. I won't go through that hell again. This time I'm getting my lifeboat. It's not going to be forever. But I have to do this. I need to know that I can take care of myself."

He wanted to hate her then, but he couldn't because for four years he had watched her build up to this: the day that Tessa Hart took a step out into the big, bad world alone. Gabe had cheered for her and encouraged her, but right now all he had was a bad morning-after taste in his mouth and a heart that couldn't take the pounding anymore.

Patience, as a virtue, was fucking overrated. "You need to be alone? You need to get your lifeboat? Fine. That can be arranged."

And Gabe walked out the door.

9

THERE WAS AN HOUR before class started, and Tessa was showered, dressed and in her room, halfway through packing, when she heard his keys in the door. Gabe was home.

Crap.

She told herself that it wouldn't matter and she continued packing, and he didn't knock, didn't say hello. He probably didn't even know she was home. However, then it was time to leave. Tessa took a deep breath and opened the door. Better to just rip this off quickly in one painful pull.

"I'm leaving," she announced to his closed door, just in case he cared.

The door opened.

"Have a nice day," he muttered, then glanced behind her, saw the suitcases. "I don't expect you to move out until your new place is ready. I may be a lot of things, but I'm not an asshole, Tessa. You should know that about me by now."

"I thought it'd be easier," she said, because she couldn't do this. Couldn't see him every day, couldn't face the disappointment in his eyes.

"And where are you going?"

She stayed silent because she also didn't have a clue.

"You don't have a place to go, do you?"

"No."

"Don't be stupid."

"I'm not stupid," she snapped. He'd never called her stupid before, and that one hurt—since it was true.

"No, you're not. Stay here. We'll deal."

"I don't think that's a good idea."

"Probably not, but it would be consistent with our track record, don't you think?"

"I'm going to go," she said, and started for the door. She didn't have time for this conversation. She now had half an hour before class started and she planned to be there early. Tessa reached out, put her hand on the door…and, yes, now Gabe started to talk.

"There're a lot of cold-blooded people in this city, but I never thought you'd be one of them. I thought I knew you. Tessa who always put people first. It's completely un-New York, and it's why I… Never mind."

"I'm sorry."

"But you'd do it again, wouldn't you? Even knowing how badly this has turned out."

She stared at the floor, stared at her newly polished toenails and her one perfect pair of shoes. "That's not fair."

"Fair? You're playing *Let's Make a Deal* with Marisa in order for you to get an apartment. That's pretty 'not fair,' Tessa.

"It was one date."

"It could have been a really good one date. It could have been the best one date ever. We could have ended up married or something."

"Then I would have had to move on."

"So are you going to answer the question?"

"What question?" she said, pretending to be stupid.

"Would you do it again?"

The sad truth was that she wouldn't do it again, not now. One week ago, when she agreed to set up Marisa with Gabe, the world was different, Gabe was different, she was different. Maybe she loved him then, but she didn't know it. Now she knew. And yeah, maybe she'd regret not having that apartment for the rest of her life, but she'd get over it.

"No, I couldn't."

"Liar."

She glared at him furiously. She had never lied—*never*—and he knew it. "Screw you, Gabe," she yelled, stamping her perfect pair of shoes, not even caring if she broke a heel. "Believe whatever the hell you want because you will never understand this. Never."

"So tell me why, Tessa. Make me understand." Gabe sat down on the couch and crossed his arms. "I've got all day."

Tessa looked at her watch, the minutes ticking past, and she hated him for making her choose, but she stayed. "I've been telling you for four years, but I don't know if you haven't been paying attention or if you just haven't understood."

"I'm paying attention now."

"Why is this so difficult? I want to be on my own. I want to have a career. I want to be independent. I don't want to depend on any anybody else but me, so if I have to be by myself again, I won't be wide-awake at three in the morning, trying to figure out how I'm going to make rent or buy food. I don't ever want to go through that again, Gabe. It sucks. I don't know if real estate will work out or not. If it doesn't, I'll try something new, and if that fails, I'll find something new, until something works out. "

"And what if you fail at real estate, Tessa? Do I stand by and wait while you try something new?"

Oh, he knew exactly where to slip the knife in, so smooth, so subtle, undermining the new shoes, the new haircut, the new Tessa. "Yes."

"That's bullshit."

And what had she expected from him? Unconditional support? Oh, yeah, right. Not in this lifetime. Not in Tessa's lifetime. "It's my reality. I can't help it if I'm complicated.

When I moved to New York I thought I could take over the world. That's what happens when you're twenty-two and really pissed off. But here I am four years later and I can't even afford to live by myself. If you want a relationship with me, Gabe, we do this on my terms—and I'm fixing myself first."

"Your terms are crap."

"What do you want?" she asked, still clinging to some piece of hope that they could make this work.

"I want you here, Tessa. Stay here. With me. Prove it. Prove that I mean more to you than your four walls, a ceiling and a part-time doorman." He looked at her from his comfortable position on his couch, in his apartment, holding her heart in his hands, and the pathetic truth was she wanted to say okay.

His eyes called to her, said that he loved her, and she knew he did. In Gabe's world, nothing would be finer than to take care of Tessa forever, and it was so tempting to give in.

She wanted to wilt and quiver and sit down next to him and pretend that they'd always be together, and she'd let him take care of her forever, too. But she knew she couldn't. She had to prove this to herself and she wouldn't let anyone take it away from her. Not even Gabe.

She raised her head, prepared for the death blow. "I can't."

The light in his eyes dimmed, then blew out entirely. It hurt, but she was still standing, and that counted for something. At the end of the day, Tessa was still standing.

Gabe nodded toward the door. "You should go. You don't want to be late for the first day of the rest of your life."

"I love you."

He laughed at her. *Laughed.*

THE FIRST DAY OF CLASS went well, considering that her love life was in the toilet. Tessa took notes, listened, aced the daily quiz and thought maybe this might work.

At the lunch break she stayed in the empty classroom, studying. Then her cell rang, and her heart stopped, thinking that maybe Gabe had changed his mind.

Alas, it was only Marisa.

"Hello, Trump-in-training. How goes it?"

"All's well," answered Tessa, lying through her teeth. Heart-ripping misery did that to a person. Made them do things they'd never consider—and she didn't even feel guilty.

"Meet me for drinks after class." Which translated to, *Let's talk about Gabe.*

"Gotta work," answered Tessa, not lying this time.

"Not a problem. I'll meet you there."

And it was no wonder Marisa was a great Realtor. She did not give up. *Ever.* "Gabe's off tonight. Poker night," Tessa told her, taking her pencil and jamming it into the composition book, making nice, punching holes in the paper. Very satisfying.

"That just means we can talk about him more. Correct?"

Tessa put down her pencil. She wanted to be a sadistic, bloodthirsty bitch, but unfortunately she couldn't do that right, either. "Correct."

Marisa hung up with a cheerful ta-ta, and Tessa went back to studying human rights and the fair-housing laws until the class resumed and the rest of the afternoon passed in a blur.

Somewhere in the two hours between liens and easements, Tessa decided that she was going to grow a spine and tell Marisa that she wanted to be with Gabe. Of course, there was the small problem that he currently wanted to wipe the memory of her from his brain—but one day at a time. And there was also the small problem that Marisa might back out of the Hudson Towers deal, but Tessa didn't think so. And if she did…well, *que sera sera,* Tessa would simply find another way to get into the building.

After class, she changed into her regular T-shirt, jeans and scruffy cowboy boots. The wonderful thing about poker night meant that it was girls' night at Prime. Lindy covered the back bar, Tessa took the front two, and by eight o'clock the seats were packed with happy customers who needed their drinks.

Tessa poured shots, she slung bottles, she flipped glasses and in general put on the show of her life.

Everybody loves a bartender.

Whatever Lindy didn't have in talent she made up for in attitude and smiles. She dropped four bottles while trying to match Tessa's double-back-twist rum-bottle flip, until Tessa intervened and decided to stop showing off so much. But it felt good. It felt good to have a skill and know that at least behind the bar, no one could touch her.

No one except for Gabe.

And that thought immediately depressed her again, restarting the whole vicious cycle of who had said what when.

Marisa came in at nine and managed to flirt her way into the front stool, trading it for her phone number.

Tessa was amazed.

"I thought you only dated bartenders."

"Please. It was a 1-900 number. Give me some credit."

Tessa took a deep breath, made ready to tell her, blended four margaritas and poured two Neutron Bombs and then took another deep breath. Courage, thy name is not Tessa.

Eventually she couldn't stall anymore. "There's something you should know."

Marisa, properly anticipating juicy gossip, leaned forward.

"Remember if you asked me if you'd be poaching on my reserves if you went out with Gabe?" stated Tessa, her voice firm. Ish.

"Yeah."

"Well, you would be. Were. Will be. Poaching. I want him," she said, waiting for Marisa to screech and jump over the bar with claws extended.

"I figured that one out," Marisa replied, which made the whole thing hugely anticlimactic.

"Really?"

"Sure. When he kissed me it was like kissing my brother or something. Don't want to go there again."

"Really? He kissed you?"

"It was very strange."

"With tongues?" asked Tessa, trying to not screech, but it was there. Screeching. Like fingernails on glass.

"No tongues. Absolutely no tongues."

"If you want to take Hudson Towers away, I'll understand."

Marisa looked at her, the smile fading. "I heard something today, Tessa."

"Bad news?" asked Tessa, her crisis radar operating at full strength.

"Depends on your point of view. The building is definitely going co-op. About three months after your move. It's all been on the hush-hush, which is why the old lady wanted to keep your sublease under the table. However, you will have the option to buy in. The good news is that my source says they'll need to replace the entire heating system within a year, so the price isn't as high as it could be. Again, they're trying to keep it hush-hush, but word gets out. People talk."

"Oh," Tessa said quietly, because was she really surprised? Things that seemed to be too good to be true always were, and she had a tattoo on her hip to prove it. But trite bumper-sticker wisdom wasn't going to help.

"Now, I don't want to get your hopes up or anything, but in three months you can probably afford it, assuming you get your license on the first pass, and if the deals go your way, which *can* be arranged because not only am I your friend but I'm also very generous. Just don't forget it twenty years from now when I call in my marker. Because after twenty years the marker could be very, very big."

"You really think I could afford it?" asked Tessa. Marisa seemed so…confident.

Marisa nodded. "The only bubble in new York is the diamond-studded one that's on display inside Tiffany's window. You'll be fine."

Fine. Tessa wasn't sure what fine felt like, but she knew that this heartache wasn't it.

"So what are you going to do?" asked Marisa, sipping elegantly on her Sidecar, which Tessa had made with an extra triple shot of brandy. Not something that she normally did, but, okay, maybe she was still nursing some unresolved feelings of hostility about Marisa's kiss with Gabe.

"About what?"

"About that," answered Marisa, pointing to Gabe's picture on the wall.

"I think he hates me. We had a huge fight."

"What about?"

"My quest for a life and his firm belief that I already have one."

"Not something that can be solved with a flip of the quarter. Can I give you some advice?"

"Could I stop you?"

"Don't even try. I think you should turn balls-out and go after him. Very Joan Collins."

Tessa slammed four shot glasses on the counter and let the tequila run free. "I'm not sure the aggressive-woman persona works well with Gabe."

Marisa frowned. "You may be right."

Lindy came forward, a glass spinning dangerously close to Tessa, until Tessa reached out a hand and plucked it from the air.

Lindy shook her head. "What are we talking about?"

Tessa glared meaningfully at Marisa. There was appropriate bar gossip and there was inappropriate bar gossip, and Gabe was completely taboo. "Nothing."

"Men," Marisa vaguely replied. She grinned encouragingly at some medical-professional type behind her, and Tessa grinned.

"You're hopeless, aren't you?" Tessa asked, but she meant it in the nicest way.

Marisa smiled back. "Yeah."

POKER NIGHT AT SEAN'S was not nearly the drunkfest that Gabe was hoping it'd be. So far, he'd only had two sips of lukewarm beer that he had no thirst for—and he was also in the hole for a cool three hundred.

It was a prizewinner of a day all round.

After his fourth losing hand, Gabe scowled at Sean. "What's the latest from City Hall?"

"Ah, yes, I'm glad you asked. Candy is looking as lovely as ever and we're having a late dinner on Sunday, so make sure I'm not working."

"The liquor license?"

"Looks to be all in order. She said that someone was asking questions, but they investigated and you're clean."

Gabe heaved a sigh of relief. At least one thing had gone right today. "The building permit?"

"Not as good. Another two weeks, but they do expect it to come through."

"So what's the holdup?"

Sean let out an exasperated sigh. "An environmental inspector. But I swear, as God is my witness, if there's a female inspector to be had, I'll find her."

Gabe swore under his breath. Still, the work on the place next door would give him something to do rather than sit in an empty apartment and be depressed. As a rule, Gabe was a happy person. Or he had been until recently.

"If you know any bartenders, I'm fixing to lose one."

Sean and Daniel looked at Cain, who held up his hands.

"Don't look at me, unless you're about to fire me because I'm winning, and that'd be really shitty Gabe. Really shitty."

"Tessa," stated Gabe. "She'll be leaving in f few weeks. I'l have to replace her."

"Tessa?" asked Daniel.

Gabe didn't like the way his brother said the name, as if i was all Gabe's fault that Tessa was leaving and that Gabe wa being a jerk. "Yes, Tessa," answered Gabe, probably a littl more jerklike than was intended. But, damn it, he was th victim here, not her.

After an additional six losing hands, Gabe shot up from hi chair and went over to the kitchen to pour himself somethin; stronger. Maybe he was unlucky at cards, unlucky at love, bu when there was nothing else left, a man could always ge lucky with Southern Comfort.

Unfortunately Daniel walked into the kitchen and caugh Gabe in midpour. "I should thank you for the other night, bu next time let's leave the strange women out of it."

"Marisa isn't strange at all." Gabe didn't like Daniel think ing that he owed him a favor, especially now that Gabe had a double shot of SoCo in his hand, which, to the undiscernin; eye, might indicate weakness. Gabe didn't like weakness i himself, because Gabe's problems were nobody else's bu Gabe's.

"She's not Tessa."

Gabe swallowed the shot, felt the burn and eyed his brothe blandly. "Tessa who?"

"Gabe, I've seen my life end badly. I'd prefer to think tha you could pull your head out long enough to right a simpl relationship tangle. Oops, forgot—you don't have much ex perience in that area, do you?"

Gabe chose to avoid all the truth in the statement, hangin; up on the detail that was wrong. "Simple? Is that what yo think this is?"

"Is she dead?" asked Daniel quietly yet effectively.

"No."

Daniel held up his hands. "Everything else is simple, Gabe. Tessa loves you."

Which would be marvelous if she didn't keep poking the serrated knives through his heart. "And now she's got an apartment she loves more."

"That's stupid."

"Sad yet true. You think I'm admitting this proudly? I wouldn't be so pissed if off it was another man. But, no, I play second string to a piece of real estate."

"So fix it. Isn't that what you like to do? Don't tell me you can't do this."

"No man should have to go through this hell for a woman. I'm done."

"Then I'll take the three thousand you owe me."

Now, after we're done, Tessa decides to tell the world that we slept together? "Tessa said something? I told her not to."

"She didn't have to. I've been waiting for four years for you and her to get on the same page."

"I'll write you a check."

Daniel swore. "Don't screw this up, Gabe. If you do, I'll have to hate you for throwing this away—and I don't want to hate you."

"She's the one who's moving out, Daniel. Talk to Tessa, not me."

10

FOR TESSA, THE NEXT ten days went by in a blur of classes and work, with a complete lack of Gabe in her life and also in his own apartment. His schedule was meticulously planned to look as though he were busy and not avoiding her. It probably would have worked except for the pertinent yet inescapable fact that they were living in the same apartment and employed at the same place.

Every morning she woke to a new note carefully taped to her door with duct tape. He was opening the bar, he was closing the bar, he was starting on the renovations, he was playing Frisbee football with Sean in the park. And every morning she crumpled the paper in a ball and threw it in the trash, especially that last one. It was ultimate in brush-offs. Sean didn't play Frisbee football, Tessa did, and Gabe knew it—and Gabe knew that Tessa knew it, too.

However, moving day was on the horizon, and every night after class she went to stand in front of Hudson Towers and stare. She learned the name of the mailman and the water delivery kid who tried to ask her out on a date, she figured out the schedule for grocery deliveries and even introduced herself to the Polish woman who ran the laundry down the street.

It was everything she'd ever wanted and yet it still felt flat. So why did Gabe have to be so stubborn? Why did men want it all, but when woman want not even half of it, then, no, it's some huge, breakup issue. To Tessa, it didn't seem fair. And the next time she got up the courage to confront Gabe, probably in the next decade, she was going to tell him so.

Class went well, a heck of a lot better than the accounting one. She aced her quizzes, she mastered the nuts and bolts of real-estate contracts. She studied insurance, taxes, commissions—and although it was a snoozer, too, Marisa assured her that the class was like popping your cherry. Painful yet necessary in order to get to the good stuff. Tessa wasn't quite sure about the correctness of that analogy, but she was optimistic.

According to Marisa, success in real estate was about fulfilling people's dreams, which Tessa bought into completely. For her, an apartment was a dream. A home, a place to call your own. To celebrate her last day of class, Marisa met Tessa for dinner, and soon, to Tessa's delight, Marisa began to talk shop, treating her just like an equal.

Over sushi, Tessa listened as Marisa complained about her first problem clients—a couple, Tom and Franklin DePaula, who were looking for a two-bedroom in Chelsea that had quick access to restaurants and laundry and was close to the number four line.

"You've shown them 457 Sixth Avenue?" asked Tessa.

"Too pretentious. These people are not very modern."

"Chelsea Gardens?"

"Yes, but they didn't like the doorman. Said that he was a little squinty-eyed."

"What about 57 West Twenty-Sixth?"

"Too expensive."

Tessa pulled at her hair, walking down the streets in her mind. "And what about the place on Twenty-Second? Where is that? Three-twenty-something, I think. It's closer to Gramercy than Chelsea, but it has the restaurants and the laundry, there's a Trader Joe's there, the price is right and, best of all, they're right at Union Square. I've heard that Marcel the doorman is a gem, and the apartments are a lot more comfortable. I bet they'd like that. A lot of couples will tell you they want Chelsea, but unless they're looking for a certain flash, comfortable trumps modern every time."

"Three-twenty-seven. Yeah, I know that building." Marisa considered it for a minute, popping a California roll in her mouth while she thought. "Not a bad idea. Give me a second." Then she pulled out her cell, and in less than two minutes flat Marisa had set up a showing. "You're coming with me, right?"

Tessa felt a quaking in her gut that had nothing to do with dinner. "I can't do that. I'm not licensed."

"Are you serious?" asked Marisa, whose gut had probably never quaked in her life, much less even tremored.

Tessa wielded her chopsticks like a weapon. "Yes. I'm supposed to have a license. And proper attire, and a positive attitude. I have none of those."

Marisa shrugged. "I don't see a problem here."

Tessa was content to finish dinner, pay out the check and let the subject drop. Which worked until they made it to the door and Tessa started in the opposite direction.

"Where do you think you're going?"

Tessa stopped, stared, and felt the entire city of New York staring at her, laughing, mocking her for even thinking that she could survive here. "Hello? I can't do it. What if you lose the deal because of me?"

"I'm not going to lose the deal because of you. That's ridiculous. First of all, you're pretty good. Second of all, I'm way better than good. Nobody walks away from Marisa Beckworth."

Tessa began to walk away, and Marisa grabbed her arm. "Was I talking to air?"

"I can't do this."

"Yes. Yes, you can. You want a career in real estate?"

Tessa licked her lips, fighting a bad case of dry mouth. This was it. Time to put up or shut up. "Yes," she spoke, her voice quivering like the mealymouthed coward she was.

"Say it like you mean it, Tessa."

"Yes," she said, firmer this time.

"Not bad. Now you're coming with me. No arguments."

"Really?" asked Tessa, starting to follow in Marisa's dog-eat-dog footsteps.

"Really."

"Okay, just try and stop me."

"That's my girl."

At the building, Tom and Franklin were thrilled. The apartment that was available looked out over a row of brownstones (so much better than those hideous concrete monstrosities on Tenth) and, best of all, Tom's dachshund had access to the dog run at Union Square Park.

Ever prepared, Marisa pulled out the application papers and a contract, as well. "When Tessa suggested Gramercy, I wasn't sure—there's not a lot of rentals there. But she knew. You're lucky that she's my friend. Now let's get the boring details out of the way. You'll need to sign these and return them by the end of the week, and then I would recommend a first month's deposit so it doesn't get snapped up."

By the time Tom and Franklin were off to the Container Store to buy closet shelving, Tessa was feeling perkier. A lot perkier.

Marisa's cell rang, and she looked at the caller ID and swore.

"Problem?"

"You don't know the half of it. Peggy's a total pain in the butt." She gave Tessa an appraising look. "Ready to move up to the majors?"

"Let me at her."

And Marisa wasn't kidding. Peggy Sanchez was a divorcée in her late fifties with a lot of money and a lot of ideas about where she wanted to live. Sadly her rental pedigree wasn't enough to get her into the top places, where she wanted to be.

So Marisa spent the evening in a pricey bar, telling Peggy that the Chamberlain was highly overrated and, yeah, movie stars lived there, but who in America wants to live in a building surrounded by the press at all hours?

Peggy was undeterred. However, Tessa had a better idea.

There was a second story apartment that would be perfect, she told her. At first, Peggy was in awe of the al fresco painted lobby and the team of discreet bellmen who handled the front desk, but things quickly went happily downhill from there.

Tessa purposely the drapes to expose the billboard advertising a seedy gentlemen's club. And right at ten o'clock, practice began, the loud bass of a Van Halen cover making the windows vibrate in four/four time. When she took Peggy on the tour of the bathroom, she made sure that Peggy's leather Manolo Blahnik's were in the flood-zone range. So as the toilet flushed, water submerged everything, including, sadly, Peggy's new Manolos.

Immediately there was much sympathy oohing and aahing as Peggy was whisked back downstairs, whereupon they bumped into a seventeen-year-old photographer stalking the latest Hollywood party girl in order to match the latest "Ready for Rehab?" headline and pay for an additional semester of his college.

Even for Peggy, it was enough, and when Marisa showed her the postwar classic six on Forty-Seventh with extra storage and a kitchen to die for, Peggy was sold.

Afterward, Marisa was curious.

"How did you know about the toilet?"

Tessa grinned. "There is no problem that duct tape cannot solve—or cause, actually. My first apartment had a major leaking problem with the stopper. Gabe showed me how to patch it with duct tape until he replaced it. Duct tape is the miracle product of the twenty-first century."

"And the band?"

Tessa pulled out her MP3 player and portable speakers. "Tunes to go."

"Gabe teach you that one, too?"

"No, I used to use it when my roommate, Hailey, got too loud with her boyfriend. Van Halen seemed to work best."

Marisa shook her head. "Keep it up. You'll almost be better than me."

"Almost? What sort of half-assed talk is that? You watch your back, sister. Tessa's here, and she's here to stay."

And she was....

MOVING DAY CAME FAST and furious in a blur of wind and rain. She'd opted to move on Friday, hoping to get out while Gabe was at work. However, for the first time in twenty-one days, her phantom roommate appeared.

She had the last boxes packed up and was hauling them into the living room when the door opened, and there was Gabe. *Would it ever get any better?* she asked herself. He was such a perfect man. There were dark splotches under the cloudy blue eyes, and he wasn't smiling, but it didn't matter. Her heart still went thump. Would she always want to throw herself at him, and wonder what the heck he was doing with a wreck like her?

"Moving out?" he asked, the master of detection.

Tessa noted the three boxes on the floor and the one suitcase and realized that even now her worldly possessions didn't amount to much. "I figured you'd want your apartment back."

"No rush," he said as if he enjoyed sleeping at his brother's and, possibly, she suspected, the bar. "Do you need help with that?"

"No, I can manage. It's not a lot."

"You can't manage the futon."

"I took it apart."

"Very smart."

"Yeah, sometimes my genius overwhelms me."

"I got something for you."

A present. Oh, that was such a low blow. They weren'
speaking, and here he was giving her a going-away present
"A roll of toilet paper and a six-pack of diet soda?"

"No." He went off to the bedroom and came back with a
small box. "I thought you could use it…you know, when you
get lonely."

Sweet. He'd bought her a vibrator. The ultimate in breakup
presents. "You didn't have to," she stammered, not wanting
to lift the lid.

Until she heard the weak meow.

Cautiously she opened the box and stared into the face of
a tiny, fuzzy kitten and felt something inside her go whoosh.
The little guy or girl had blue-gray eyes that nearly matched
the color of Gabe's. Tessa suspected that was unplanned.

"You didn't have to," she said, lifting the small cat out of
the box and holding it close. "Is it a girl or a boy?"

"I got a boy. For protection." Gabe's mouth was pulled into
a tight line, not the normal curve, and she wondered if she'd
ever see him smile again.

"He looks tough," she offered. "Does he have a name?"

"According to the SPCA, he's called Fluffy. I thought you
could come up with something better than that."

"Caesar, I think. He looks very tough."

Gabe examinied the kitten skeptically. "Whatever. I bor-
rowed Cain's truck because I'm assuming you didn't make ar-
rangements?"

Tessa looked at him with newly mastered arrogance and
actual self-confidence. "I've seen people with a mattress on
the subway."

"Come on. You can take the girl out of Florida, but you
can't take the Florida out of the girl."

She whacked him on the arm. "I think you just insulted the
entire population of the fourth largest state in America."

He looked down at his arm, stared, and the moment was

gone. It was official: they were over. And now she had a kitten and a brand-new apartment to prove it.

GABE WASN'T SURE WHAT he'd expected when he entered Tessa's new apartment. Possibly the eighth ring of hell, possibly some HGTV nightmare with flowers and lots of froufrou wallpaper. Actually, it was okay.

"Not bad," he said, which was about as complimentary as he was willing to be.

"It's perfect. I told you." Immediately she launched into the benefits of the place, pointing out the fine detail in the carpentry, the one extra outlet in the living area, the spacious (eight-by-nine) bedroom and the above-average closet space. Although she omitted mention of the nasty crack in the ceiling, which Gabe hoped wasn't an indicator of a shoddy foundation.

Still, Tessa wanted this place, and that should count for something. Gabe stood by, hands locked behind his back, and maybe Gabe needed the time to get his brain attuned to the truth of things. The truth was that Tessa needed this, and since the day she'd walked into Prime with her shell-shocked eyes, Gabe had always known that this was her end point. Okay, maybe not Hudson Towers specifically but getting out on her own, proving that she could.

Gabe wanted to stand by her, be the cool friend that she needed, but that involved patience and understanding, and Gabe had gotten all tapped out recently. It was probably the sleeping with her that had sucked it all dry.

Now all he could think about was having her back in his bed, holding her close and knowing she'd be there when he got home at four in the morning from Prime. He and Tessa belonged together. As soon as Tessa realized that being alone was a suck-ass proposition, she'd come back.

And Gabe would be waiting.

For that, he could hold out on anything. Including her. He watched as she picked up the kitten and smiled.

HER FIRST NIGHT ALONE in her new place. Tessa ordered in Chinese and cranked up Cher while Caesar curled up in her lap. She was missing the chintz chair, but that would come in time. In another few weeks she'd start making some commissions and in the interim her bartending tips would cover it.

Listening to music, feeling Caesar purr against her legs, she sat wondering what Gabe was up to. She turned off the CD player and picked up her cell.

"What are you doing?"

"Cutting wood," he answered, his voice cautious.

"Where are you, Oregon?"

"Next door to Prime."

And suddenly the picture became clear. Gabe was doing all the work on the renovations himself in the spare four hours of his time. Tessa checked the clock and sighed, making sure that he heard it. "It's nine o'clock at night."

"I'm sorry, but my little elves are union guys and are contractually forbidden from working after five."

"Oh." Next time she saw Sean and Daniel, she was going to have a long, long chat about how they couldn't leave this up to Gabe. He'd work himself to death.

"How's the new place?" he asked.

"Good," she replied just as Caesar walked up her arm to curl in a newfound spot around her neck.

"Good is good."

"Gabe?"

"Yeah?"

Tessa took a deep breath and threw her self-respect to the wind. "Maybe you could take a break later?" There it was: *the booty call.*

There was a long, long silence. Tessa waited, her self-respect trying to figure out if it'd gone kamikaze for nothing. "I've got a lot of work to do here," he finally responded.

Which meant no. "Oh," she said, not bothering to hide her disappointment. Her first booty call—and her first rejection. She'd never practiced this before, mainly because when you have a roommate, the call was awkward and weird and usually too much trouble. But now? She had freedom. But freedom to receive rejection really sucked eggs.

"Tessa?" he said, and her heart perked up at the change in his tone.

"Yes?" She hoped, hoped, hoped he was reassessing his rejection.

"This was your idea. Give yourself a chance."

Nope. No reassessment. She was still rejected. So Tessa brought out the big guns. "You're going to make me pull out my vibrator?"

"Damn!" he yelled into the phone, and even Caesar jumped from his perch on Tessa's shoulder.

"Gabe!"

"Sorry, I just hammered my finger," he answered, which made her feel rejected, guilty and yet secretly pleased that the thought of her with a vibrator caused him physical injury. Oh, God, she was a sadist.

"Sorry. I should go," she said, because this was all more complicated than it was supposed to be.

"I'll see you tomorrow."

Tomorrow? Twenty-four hours? Tessa could handle that. It wasn't a rejection as much as it was a temporary restraining order. "Really?"

"Really. You're supposed to work at seven."

"Oh."

He laughed then, an evil laugh, as if he knew the pain she would be going through, after which Tessa promptly hung up on him.

And pulled out her brand-spanking-new vibrator.

Sadly four years of great expectations did not live up to the hype. Not even close.

Mainly because it wasn't Gabe.

11

THE NEXT DAY, TESSA got conned into shopping with Lindy, who had the sleaziest taste in clothes of anyone that Tessa knew. At first Tessa said no. Sleazy wasn't her style, it wasn't her look and, also, if you dressed for sex and men said no, well, what good was that? However, Lindy had something she wanted to talk about, and Tessa figured, yeah, maybe there was something to dressing for sex. Pathetic? Check. Desperate? Check. Already tossed the vibrator in the trash? Check.

Lindy took her into four stores that were somewhat more extreme than Tessa had been hoping for. There were microskirts, red velvet bustiers and lace shirts that wouldn't cover a shot glass, not that Tessa's breasts were much bigger than shot glasses, but still—no. No, no, no.

Eventually Tessa felt the need to clarify the purpose of this shopping extravaganza. She put back the lace shirt that Lindy was holding up to her in a hopeful manner. "You said you need to talk, not send me out in the streets to make a living."

With a regretful shake of her head, Lindy replaced the lace shirt. "You're making a really big mistake by not going for the lace. It's completely you."

"In what universe? Talk!"

"I think I'm going to move back home. To Trenton. I don't think I can afford the city anymore, and Peter wants me to come back."

Tessa's jaw dropped open. "Peter? You mean Peter actually exists?"

"Yeah. He was my ex. He said he still loved me and he knew that I'd never make it. And you know something? He was right."

Oh, God. Tessa didn't need to hear that. Of course Peter was wrong. "You can't give up, Lindy. Who's going to dress me?"

"You don't need me anymore, Tessa. Look at you. My little girl has grown up. All polished, and you have a real career, and I suspect you have a secret man in your life—which would make that bar pool rigged. Not that I'm saying anything, just saying."

"You're leaving me at Prime? Alone?" Tessa looked around the clothes store and wished for a strong shot of tequila instead of fishnet hose. "Have you told Gabe?"

"A few days ago," she answered, and Tessa realized that Gabe hadn't said a word to her. No surprise.

"You made your mind up? Nothing I can do to change it?"

"Barring a winning lottery ticket, nah, I think I'm settled on a new path. You're a good friend, even if your belly button isn't pierced. You're always going to be my hero, Tessa."

A hero. Tessa had never been anything close to somebody's hero. The thought warmed her, although that could have been the summer heat. And she didn't feel heroic, she felt slightly bitchy, with a nervous instinct to pull at her hair. Heroic was something new. She gave Lindy a ninety-pound-weakling smile. "Get me something crazy to wear before you make me cry."

Several hours later they were no closer to success. Lindy put a thumb between her teeth and considered Tessa's jeans with a hole in the knee (which at one time was considered very high fashion, Tessa reminded her) and the plain Hanes T-shirt.

"I know the perfect place," she blurted and whisked Tessa down to a hole-in-the-wall garage off the West Side Highway.

"What is this dump?" asked Tessa, taking in the corrugated metal walls and the spray-painted graffiti—and the significant absence of people.

"It's my connection," said Lindy and then pressed the red buzzer on the wall. A metal door in the back opened and a postapocalyptical punk type of androgynous sex walked through.

"Carlos," said Lindy, raising one fist in greeting.

"What's up, bitch?" he asked without a trace of hostility, and Tessa watched the interchange, fascinated.

"I need some leather, Carlos."

Instantly Tessa stopped breathing. "I don't need leather."

Lindy laughed. "The leather. Something leggy, boot cut. Probably not black, though. Brown, I think."

"I can't afford leather pants," whispered Tessa.

"You want to make a statement?"

"Yes?" Tessa could hear the nervous quiver in her voice. "Yes," she answered again, this time sans quiver.

Lindy arched one brow in a question.

"I'm going to do this," announced Tessa, realizing that, yes, it was getting easier after all.

IT TOOK A LOT FOR TESSA to get ready for work that night. Lindy was appointed chief stylist, and Caesar sat on the toilet tank, mewing at the appropriate moments. There was much brushing, plucking, spraying, moussing, padding and even exfoliating.

Finally it was time for the unveiling. Lindy removed the towel that covered the mirror and let Tessa look.

"Wow," she said, not ready to commit to more than that. Okay, she looked good. No, she looked great. The hair was perfect, the brows were perfect, the liner was a bit darker than usual, but it looked nice, sexy.

"This is not just 'wow,'" said Lindy, defending her work product.

"Wow," repeated Tessa, unable to come up with anything better. It was her and yet…not. While she was still contemplating the woman in the mirror, Lindy took Tessa's Prime shirt, and cut off the midriff and the sleeves.

Tessa shook her head, realizing that resistance was futile. "Gabe will have a fit."

"All the guys will have a fit. That's the idea, right? Trust me, anything that makes the customers happy will make Gabe happy."

Looking at the face in the mirror, the cropped shirt, and with the idea of Gabe in mind, Tessa felt the acid boiling over in her stomach. "Lindy, I don't think this is right."

"It's better than right. It's fab. You look fab. Très confident, très daring, très bold. It's the new and improved Tess. Put it on," she said, holding the shirt out as if it was Pandora's box.

Maybe Lindy new what she was doing. Tessa wanted Gabe back in her bed, and the usually weakling Tessa hadn't worked, so maybe this was the answer. And how bad did she want him? *Bad.*

Tessa had wanted to recharge her life, and a crop top with leather pants didn't seem crazy outrageous. Much. She put on the shirt and the pants and then finished it off with her red high-tops. Tessa eyed them, not quite sure they added to the whole life-recharge moment.

Lindy gushed before Tessa could say a word. "Leave them. It's eclectic, serendiptious and makes you look self-assured."

"As opposed to stupid?"

"Not stupid at all."

Tessa gave herself one last look in the mirror. "Whatever you say."

GABE'S SATURDAY NIGHT started out badly and seemed to go downhill from htere. The plumber had shown up to work next door, had asked to see the building permit and, when Gabe explained the situation, had promptly disappeared. One of the beer distributor's trucks had crashed on the L.I.E, and they were running on beer foam for the night. And the health inspector (male this time) decided to show up for a surprise visit.

All in all, he thought it couldn't get any worse, until nine o'clock, when Tessa showed up for work. She walked through the door, and Gabe didn't look up, not until he heard Sean's patented wolf whistle. He looked up, then went back to pouring drinks, and then two seconds later his brain registered what his eyes had.

That was Tessa?

Holy shit.

Immediately Sean hopped over the bar and came to propel her forward, turning her around just so he could study her leather-encased ass.

"Tessa, my darling," Sean purred, and Gabe, not one to practice violence with his brothers, considered planting a fist in Sean's way-too-happy face.

Gabe didn't want to look, he didn't want to leer, he didn't want to ogle and, most importantly, he did not want to drool, but he couldn't help it.

Little Tessa Hart was playing dirty, dirty pool, and Gabe, for a moment forgetting his high-minded plans to hold out on her, found himself fascinated.

Sean, who never did work for anyone but himself, filled her ice bin, hefted a case of beer, and in general situated himself right under her thumb.

Gabe didn't want to glare. He couldn't help it.

"Problem?" Tessa asked him oh-so-sweetly.

"No problem," snapped Gabe, pulling a bottle of whiskey, flipping it into the air and promptly dropping it.

She snickered.

Tessa continued to be the focus of all male attention in the bar, and she was eating it up. He could tell. She was always smiling, pouring shots with a flourish, shaking mojitos and, yes, everything else along with them.

Worst of all, Sean—Gabe's brother who would jump anything female that wore tight leather pants—was in love.

Gabe wanted to ignore her, he really did, but his eyes kept creeping back to her body, the trim expanse of skin at her waist that exactly fit his hands. And the leather. Good gawd, who knew that leather was so cock-stiffening?

By eleven o'clock he was suffering from a clear case of blue balls and he stalked downstairs, mainly to give himself a break.

Sadly Tessa happened to choose that moment to go downstairs, as well. "You're mad," she stated, possibly noticing the pulsing jaw, the clenched teeth and the three bottles that he'd dropped that night.

"I'm not mad."

"I thought you'd like me like this."

Actually, he liked her like this. He liked her like this, and part of him knew that only a moron would be giving her this much grief for something that was obviously done for his benefit. But Gabe suspected that darker forces were at work inside him. Namely the intense fear that every single day as Tessa was getting more capable, more confident, more, well, hot, her Gabe-need quotient was declining exponentially. For four years she had needed Gabe and no one else. At this rate, in less than fourteen days he'd be written out of the picture entirely. And that made Gabe scared shitless. So he ended up mad.

"Do you see how they're looking at you, Tessa?" he asked instead of *You don't need me anymore,* but she was smart now, she could figure it out on her own.

"I don't really care how anybody else looks at me but you."

Which made him feel like even more of a moron, which only made him madder. Finally, rather than trying to communicate, he elected to run back upstairs to the safety of the bar.

There he could pour drinks, flirt with like-minded females and in general postpone any emotional analysis until after closing.

Which lasted for another hour, until Sean came over. "Bet you're just aching because she didn't look like that when she was living with you, aren't you?"

"You're such an ass, Sean." God, Gabe hated relationships. He hated the uncertainty, he hated the analysis, he hated the interference and, goddammit, he hated this erection that was threatening to kill him.

"I think more people should be honest in this world. I try to call 'em like I see 'em. Everybody else is so worried about pretense. Not me."

Gabe glared. "The whole nonpretense honesty thing would be more effective if you weren't such a jerk. Sometimes it pays to make yourself look better."

"I can afford to be the bigger man. I understand your frustration. She moves out of your apartment, and this is what we get? Damn, Gabe, you are one foolish human being. You should've jumped all over that like—the bet!"

Sean turned down the music and rang the bell. "For all those customers who participated in our monthly cash-fueled, yet completely legal bar pool, I'm happy to announce that we do have a winner in the bet. If my memory serves me correct, and I believe it does, the answer to the question, when will Gabe actually get some from his roommate—pardon me, ex-roommate—is Hell Freezes Over, from Tessa Hart," he said, giving Gabe a disgusted look. "You are such a fool," he added, not helping the situation.

Tessa, to her credit, looked ready to crawl into a hole.

Sean took an envelope from the register and handed it to her. "Darlin', you earned it."

But Tessa kept pushing the money back toward Sean. "I can't take this." She looked to Gabe for help, but Gabe decided to shrug in a completely unhelpful manner.

Eventually Gabe realized that, no, Tessa actually did still need his help—which cheered him up some—and he nodded to her. "Just take it."

The rest of the night went well, and he managed to avoid any sort of confrontation until after last call. Maybe it wasn't smart to pick an argument at three in the morning, after working for pretty much twelve hours straight, all with a painful hard-on, but, yeah, there you have it. Parts of him were rubbed raw from watching her work and watching all the men fall all over her.

He saw Tessa coming downstairs with a case of wine. Her hips were moving, her hair was bouncing back and forth, and it was the world's biggest turn-on to a man with two-twenty volts running through his veins already. Gabe pulled the case from her hands and stacked it with the others. "You're doing this to make me hurt, aren't you?"

"Is it working?" she asked. "I can relieve all that pain for you." Her words were completely lacking in sympathy, which helped neither the raw pain in his heart nor his hard-on.

"No," he told her—again, not the smartest moment in his life, but he'd be damned if he was going to be suckered into this so easily. Gabe was noble, he was high-minded, he had scruples and he would not be swayed by sexual favors, because painful as it was, there was a principle at stake here. He wasn't easy, and Tessa needed to see that, too.

"How long are you going to make me pay?" she asked.

"This was your idea, not mine."

"Not the not sleeping together. That was all yours, buddy."

"You said it was—" he held up quote fingers '—not smart.' Do you remember that? You wanted to be smart, Tessa."

"Why do you listen to me?" she asked sadly, so unsure, so much like the old Tessa that he had to smile.

"You should be able to figure that one out."

Tessa stood there in hot leather pants, with buff arms and a slow grin turning up the corners of that sultry mouth.

"Can you kiss me at least? Or did I tell you that kissing was off limits, too?"

Now, Gabe might be a principled man, but there were limits to his principles. He backed her against the wall until they were chest to chest, thigh to thigh. Then softly he kissed her, holding back exactly all of the passion that was bottled up inside him, ready to explode.

When he pulled away, Tessa opened her eyes, disbelieving.

"That's it?" she asked and then grabbed his T-shirt, and he swore he heard it rip. She planted one on him, a teeth-shattering, ball-busting, tongue-lashing lesson in mouth-to-mouth. Then she walked off, perky butt swaying in leather.

Ten minutes later, Sean found him still standing in the same spot. "Anything you'd like to explain to me, Gabe?"

Gabe shook his head and pulled the ice bucket away from his cock. "I wouldn't know where to start."

TESSA'S LIFE WAS GOING okay. She was done with the classes; she only had the exam on Tuesday to pass. She was living on her own. She had a cat. And, best of all, there was Gabe, who was not apathetic to her, although he wasn't sleeping with her, either.

But first things first. Tessa was going to be a real-estate agent. And because she was absolutely, positively, one hundred percent psyched to pass this sucker with an A, she started studying at seven in the morning, and other than falling asleep during the contracts chapter, she managed fine until her cell range at eleven. Caller ID said it was her brother.

Wonderful.

"Yes?"

"Mom said you moved again."

"Into my own place, yes," Tessa exclaimed, needing to interject the important Tessa-life-altering part into the conversation.

"Been broken into yet?"

"No."

"Sink stopped up yet?"

"No."

"Neighbors partying too loud yet?"

Tessa yawned. "No."

"Okay, then, sounds great."

"Thank you, darling brother. Why are you calling?"

"Can't I just call to talk to my favorite sis?"

Which meant problems. "Why are you calling?"

Silence.

"Robert?"

"It's Denny. They got married today, Tessa. And I was afraid that Cathy or Maureen would call you and tell you and be all mean about it and I didn't want you to get hurt."

Tessa stayed quiet, gauging the emotions jockeying inside her. There was anger, there was busted pride, but there was no hurt. No hurt at all. This time Tessa didn't hurt. Another excellent point for the Tessa conversion, she was happy to note.

"I hope it works out for him," she said.

"You mean that?"

"Yes. Yes, I do. I mean that. I hope this new girl makes him happy and he finds everything that he's looking for." Wow. It all sounded humane—and, best of all, she did mean it.

"Super. I really wasn't expecting that. I thought you'd be all, you know, balling and sniveling."

"I've never done balling and sniveling."

"Not in public, but we knew. Every time you closed your door and cranked up Nirvana on the stereo, it was a dead giveaway that something was wrong."

"I'm hanging up on you now."

"Cranking up the Nirvana?"

"Nope. Cranking up the Cher. Next week—Monday, to be precise—I'm calling you back, Robert. And I'll have news. New York State officially sanctioned good news."

"You're getting married, too?"

Trust her brother to deflate great things into mediocrity. "No, not that kind of news. Career news, money news, life news, important things."

"Tessa? This isn't Tessa, is it? This is some clone that's taken over her body?"

"Nope."

"Coolness, sis."

"Night, Robert."

Tessa hung up the phone and waited for the Denny aftershocks to hit, but there were no aftershocks. She jammed up the volume on Cher, and did the happy dance for about fifteen minutes until her downstairs neighbor pounded on the ceiling.

Oh, well. She was supposed to be studying anyway.

12

ON TUESDAY TESSA PASSED the New York State real estate exam with ninety-seven percent. It was a high moment in her life, but sadly there was no one there to appreciate the achievement and share in a celebratory high-five. So as soon as she got out of the building, she popped out her cell to call Gabe. Maybe they weren't having sex, but they were on speaking—albeit frosty—speaking terms.

However, instead of a live human voice, she got the answering machine. And, even worse, Gabe's answering machine wasn't a recorded human voice but a recorded computer voice. She elected not to leave a message and instead changed into shorts and a tank top and went to find him.

While she walked past the condos that stocked the Upper East Side, she called Marisa, talking in a loud enough voice that all the apartment residents going in and out were aware that, yes, she, Tessa Hart, was now a licensed agent and available for hire.

Marisa told her to meet her at the office in four hours, after her two showings and as soon as she got the McMullens' paperwork turned in at the title company. Four hours was just enough time to search out one missing Gabe O'Sullivan. He wasn't at Prime, but the drilling noise coming from the space next door was a sure bet.

Tessa peeked in the window and took a few private minutes to watch Gabe work. Faded blue jeans, a long-sleeved denim shirt hung unbuttoned down his front, tempting a female to stop and admire the scenery. The back of his shirt was wet with sweat, and his hair was two shades darker than normal, yet Tessa could feel her body rev, ready to answer the untamed call of the working man. What was it about a sweaty man that could make a woman's mouth water? Because there was definitely mouthwatering going on here.

Tessa wished she had the right to walk in and touch and take, but Gabe was still holding out on her—and, to be frank, she wasn't sure that it was smart to surprise a man with a power drill in his hand. And lately, Tessa was all about being smart—which reminded her of exactly why she was here.

She walked in, posed in the doorway, prepared to make the grand entrance. However, due to said drilling noise, Gabe didn't even look up.

Tessa advanced two steps, posed again, and this time he noticed. The drilling stopped.

"Yes?"

She gave him her best smile. "Tessa Hart, one of the few, the proud, the licensed New York State real-estate agents."

His face cracked into a tightly restrained smile. "Congratulations. Not that I'm surprised."

She eyed the drill in his hand and told herself not to worry. "I'm surprised you're not surprised."

"You should believe in yourself more, Tessa."

She started to pull at the lock of her hair, caught herself and then nodded. "You're right. And when you're right, you're right."

"I'm always right."

"Don't get cocky." She looked around, noticed the cut lumber, the smell of sawdust in the air, and the wood shavings in his hair, which her fingers itched to brush away. But she suspected he would flinch, and she didn't want to see that because it would hurt too much. "Whatcha doing?"

"Building."

"Whatcha building?"

"A back bar. I'm doing the frame for the shelves and the facing, and then Cain promised to carve the trim for me."

"Need some help?" she asked innocently, as if she really wasn't trying to wheedle back into most-favored-person status.

"No," he answered and then started drilling again, a slapdown for her wheedling if she ever heard one. She eyed the circuit box, saw the outlets in place and started pulling wire. Gabe looked up, saw what she was doing and stopped drilling.

"What are you doing?"

"Helping."

He pulled the crimpers from her hand. "I don't expect you to do this, Tessa."

Tessa grabbed the tool back. "Would you do the same for me?"

"Yeah. But I'm a guy."

"Shut up and drill, Gabe. I'm going to let that slide, only because I'm still trying to get back on your good side, and taking time out to point to the errors in your Neanderthalesque thinking would defeat my devious yet softhearted purpose."

He stood silently, considering her, and she could see the doubt still in his eyes and she wished that he didn't doubt her. Two months ago Tessa would have simply put the crimpers down and not pressed the issue, but now she knew what she was capable of.

More importantly, she knew that she wasn't capable of squat unless she tried.

Eventually he gave her a nod. One tiny incline of the head, but hope was a powerful thing, and Tessa felt her spirits shoot through the roof.

For two hours she worked, and although she wasn't as fast, as good or probably as optimized as Gabe, by the end of it, she had three boxes done and was well on her way to making master electrician.

He examined her work, and she waited with bated breath to hear the final verdict.

Gabe nodded. "Not bad. Ready for some champagne? I think there's an old bottle down in the walk-in."

"Champagne? What are we celebrating?"

"To your new career."

Tessa nodded. It wasn't to their new relationship, but she'd take the victories where she could. "I'll drink to that."

GABE TOOK TWO GLASSES and the bottle of champagne, and they climbed up on the fire escape outside to drink. When Gabe had been a kid, working at O'Sullivan's during the summer, he and his uncle had often come up here and discussed the bar business. Patrick would talk about the future, talk about the customers and be the dad that Gabe's actual dad never was. For Gabe, there was very little better than sitting outside, watching the city move and knowing that this was your place. Tessa was finding her own place, and although he didn't like her methods, he had to give her marks for going after it.

Although, now she was going to put in her notice, he'd have to hire somebody to replace her, and Tessa wasn't easily replaced. Tessa would never be replaced. Sadly, every time she looked up at him with those wide green eyes, he wanted to abandon all his principles and say screw it—or, more accurately, screw *her.*

She leaned back against the cracked black metal railing with a contented sigh. When she sat there in an old Yankees tank and cutoffs and a splotch of grime on her cheek, his heart bumped uncomfortably. She probably would never realize how difficult it was for him to adjust to the two Tessas that were now in his life. He wanted the old one back, but he couldn't bear to see the new one fail, either.

"You come to this dive often?" she asked.

"The view's not perfect, but anytime you get to sit and see a blue sky in Manhattan it's a moment to be cherished."

He uncorked the champagne with an expert's hand and poured her a glass. "To your new career," he said, trying to keep happy, cheery thoughts in his heart, but it wasn't easy.

"Thanks," she said and clinked her glass to his.

He wasn't ready to drink, only wanted to watch her for a minute, capture the picture in his head, because he wasn't sure he'd ever see it again. "You're going to have to get some new clothes for work."

She nodded with no trace of fear in her eyes. The old Tessa would have been terrified at the thought of clothes shopping. "Marisa's going to take me out next week. We have it all planned. She told me exactly what I need to buy."

"Better Marisa than Lindy. You can afford all this?"

Tessa took another sip, and then sneezed. "Yeah. It's amazing how much less expensive the world is without college."

"Making all the bills okay?"

"Yes, Gabe, I'm holding up fine. I'm going to put in my notice," she said.

"Yeah, I figured." He knew this was coming, but even the advance notice of her notice hadn't made it easier. Slowly she was pulling out all the nails that had been the old part of her life, and Gabe knew he was the last nail left. He sighed, studied her and worried.

At least here he could keep an eye out for her, make sure things were okay for her and that she didn't need help. "If you need a loan or need your job back or something, let me know."

"I don't need you to take care of me anymore."

And what could he say to that? That's what he was afraid of? Every time he heard those four words—*I don't need you*—it really didn't matter what came after them. Gabe had made his spot in her life for him and he didn't like being evicted

rom it. He kept his mouth shut, sipped champagne and
ibsorbed the sun.

"I guess the money from the bet is helping out," he said,
iliding it right in there smoothly, his mouth not quite follow-
ng the keep-it-shut directive.

"I didn't keep it." She stretched her slim, tanned legs out
n front of her. He remembered those legs, remembered them
ocked around him, and tried to remember why he was
iolding out on her. Oh, yeah—stupidity.

"You gave the money to Daniel?" he asked, jerking himself
)ack into the present.

"He wouldn't take it. I gave it to a guy on the street."

"What the hell? Tessa, that was three thousand dollars.
You could've used it."

She shook her head. "He looked hungry. I thought it
would help."

For some reason, it irked him even more that she had no
icruples about selling him to get an apartment, but take a bet that
ihe didn't honestly win? Oh, that she couldn't do. Now she'd
urned into Saint Tessa? He took another long sip of champagne.

"Did you hire a new bartender yet?" she asked, and he was
relieved at the change of subject.

"I found one that might work out if Sean doesn't chase her
off. She's fast, makes a smooth martini, and moved here from
North Dakota a few months ago."

"She sounds perfect," Tessa commented, frowning.

"Actually, she is," said Gabe.

"Can't wait to meet her," she said, but those usually serene
green eyes weren't happy. It would have been a small-minded
and insecure man who would have been glad to see her
jealous. Gabe tried really hard not to be glad. Really hard.
Really, really hard. Okay, he was glad.

"Gabe?"

"Yes?"

"I'm going to miss working here."

"That real-estate gig should keep you all hot and bothered," he answered, which sounded both horny and noble all at the same time. Damn, he'd been going for noble, but watching her with the sun beating down on her thin cotton shirt and tiny drops of sweat glistening on bare thighs...well, hell.

"Real estate does not get me hot."

"Not even a little?" he asked, abandoning all pretense of noble. Jeez, he was turning into Sean.

"You want to know what gets me hot, Gabe?" she asked in a husky, sex-kitten voice that shot straight to his cock.

"You want to tell me now, when we're in front of eight million New Yorkers? Or do you want to tell me later, when you can just show me instead?"

She squirmed against the railing, her nipples visibly perking under her shirt, which he ached to touch. So much for holding out. Fine, where Tessa was concerned, he was whipped. And with the way she looked at him, as if he were the cherry in her Manhattan, the sloe gin in her Alabama Slammer and the sugar in her whiskey sour, he might as well admit the truth..

"Come home with me."

She didn't have to ask him twice.

WHEN THEY GOT TO HER apartment, Gabe had high plans for a shower, and a slow, soft seduction that could last for a lifetime, but the moment they got in the door Tessa changed his mind.

Thankfully.

She backed him against the table, gave him a hot, wet kiss that stopped his heart, and then the clothes were gone in record time. She climbed up on top of him, wrapping those gleaming legs around his waist, her eyes dark.

Then he pushed inside her and, damn...

This was Tessa. He wanted to concentrate on sex, wanted

o find blind pleasure, but all his heart could do was remind
im that this was the single, one woman on the planet who he
oved. Who he'd always loved.

Gabe heard himself sigh like a fool.

Why couldn't they be like this all the time? Why did she
ave to choose everything else but him?

What was wrong with the Gabe choice?

He pushed and pushed, the ache in his heart getting waylaid
y the simple pleasure of sex, and for a moment he concen-
rated on her, his hand searching, finding her sweet spot, and
e wanted her to see only him. Wanted her to want only him.
Wanted her to forget everything but him. Just this one time.
Or maybe forever.

His fingers stroked her as he moved in and out of her, and
e didn't think about tomorrow or the next day, right now he
ust wanted to kiss away her sighs, make her green eyes go
lind and somehow convince her that no freaking apartment,
o prissy desk job, nothing else could be better than this. Her
ingernails raked across his chest, and he didn't care. He
vanted her like this.

Desperate for him.

Her legs slid around his waist, her head moving back and
orth, and he kept on, his cock driving home. His hands
troked her clit, feeling her shudder each time he touched.
This time he was leaving nothing to chance.

"Please," she begged, but he wanted more and so he kept
p the torment, his muscles tight because he wanted to let go,
e wanted to grind inside her until he couldn't feel anything
ut her. Her words turned into whimpers, and all the while she
egged, meeting him thrust for powerful thrust. He knew he
vas close, knew he couldn't last much longer, but he wanted
ne win. Wanted one moment in time when she knew abso-
utely nothing in her world but him.

So, he drove her until she was shaking, gasping, her eyes

faded to dark. And when she screamed, when he knew that there was absolutely nothing for him but this, then he let himself go, and the moment disappeared.

Now back to your regularly scheduled new-and-improved Tessa programming.

He pulled out, not ready to face her, and went to get cleaned up. She met him in the shower and once again the sex was great. Abso-fucking-lutely perfect. She whispered against his back that she loved him, and he should have told her that he loved her, too, but the marks on his chest were raw and red. And ultimately she still had another man's name tattooed on her perfect ass. Most awful of all, buried underneath, Gabe's heart still hurt.

13

HE GOT DRESSED in the bedroom and could see the caution signs in her eyes. She hadn't expected silence from him. She expected him to beg, grovel, confess that he couldn't live without her—which he couldn't—but this time it was her move, it was her time to fix things. He was tired of trying.

The kitten padded into the room, watched Gabe with big eyes, and Tessa smiled.

"He likes you."

"Yeah, I saved him from a life behind bars. It's gratitude, nothing more."

"I'm getting the tattoo off tomorrow," she told him, and he shrugged casually, acting as if it was no big deal.

"You glad to get rid of it?"

"How'd you like to have *Sherry* tattooed on your butt?"

"A perfect ass shouldn't be marked," he answered.

"You got a perfect butt, Mr. O'Sullivan?"

He found himself smiling as he watched her dress; maybe there was hope after all. How long could a lease last? Six months or a year? Okay, he could last a year. Then she'd come back home. The cat pawed at his jeans, and he figured the cat could come, too. It'd be like their own little family.

In the middle of his muddled thinking, the phone rang, and he watched, waiting. But, yes, Tessa picked it up, mouthing the word *Marisa*.

Six months, Gabe reminded himself. He could wait that long.

Tessa looked at Gabe, watching him with a nervous gaze. "Thirty minutes?" she said, happy, perky. "Sure. I can make that."

She hung up on Marisa and turned to Gabe, who now had her attention for all of thirty minutes or less. Okay, not mad. Not mad. The world wanted a piece of Tessa now, and he was going to have to adjust.

He didn't want to have thirty minutes or less. "See you tonight," he told her and walked toward the door.

"Really?" she asked.

"Really. You're supposed to work at seven."

"Oh," she answered, but he didn't laugh because the joke wasn't funny anymore.

THE COCORAN OFFICE WAS located on the West Side. It hummed with activity, phone calls and conversations. Tessa met the vice president, the director of sales, four brokers and the secretary, Pauline. This was going to be her job, this was going to be her career. It was scary yet awesome all at the same time. That was the great thing about day one: no failures as of yet.

Marisa even presented Tessa with business cards. Business cards! Marisa explained about the phones and the schedules, gave her a file of listings to study and basically overwhelmed her, but in a good way. By the end of it, Tessa knew that she could do this. The listings were buildings she knew like the back of her hand, and the clients were just a matter of finding the perfect home for people.

Gabe was right.

Gabe.

This afternoon had been everything she'd wanted it to be, but Gabe had held something back from her. He wasn't happy. She knew he wasn't happy, and she knew what he wished for, but she looked around the office, looked at the faces of all those people who had everything they wanted, and she knew that she wanted that, too.

THAT AFTERNOON TESSA WENT with Marisa and a client to look at a forty-story building in Columbus Circle, and everything went fine. That night at work she met the new bartender, Jennifer, and realized the paragon woman already had a crush on Gabe. Did it have to be that way? Did every woman in America really have to crush on her man?

Her man.

Yeah, he was her man.

Tessa acted nice, showed Jen the ropes, and made her practice mojitos until Sean came over and made Tessa stop. Very sad when Sean was the one who had to remind her how to behave.

Gabe didn't notice.

That night she went home alone, looked over client requests, and complained to her kitten about men. Caesar, who was also a male, was absolutely no help, but he did make her feel loved. And that's what she missed. She wanted to feel loved again.

She worked out her two weeks' notice at Prime and every now and then Gabe would come over, have sex and then leave. She considered asking him to spend the night, but she felt as though that was a betrayal to her new independent status. And the tattoo scars on her butt still hadn't faded, either.

At the bar, no one except Daniel knew they were sleeping together, which, the way Gabe was acting, was easier than Tessa would have expected.

Marisa knew, and Tessa pretended all was well, because Tessa was turning into a really great pretender. Tessa whizzed through the six-week internship program, and by the end of the trial period she was already making more than Marisa had predicted.

Tessa was that good.

Yes, it was true. When it came to finding other people's residential happiness, Tessa was a miracle worker. One day, after closing a respectably sweet deal on the Upper West Side, Marisa and Tessa had a celebratory facial at Bliss.

"You're going to buy your apartment, aren't you?" asked Marisa tightly as her face coagulated into a solid cast.

"Do you think I should?"

"Hello? You're in the real estate biz now. Do you know the return on investment we're talking about here?"

In fact, Tessa did. "Probably."

"You'd be stupid not to, Tessa. To be fair, I wasn't sure exactly how you'd do financially—but, honey, you're cleaning up. A few mac-and-cheese nights until your commission level is bumped up in a few months, and you'll be sitting pretty as the owner of a genuine prewar, one-full-bedroom, one-bath apartment in the building that's best described as 'desirable.' Have you talked to Gabe?"

And there was a conversation that Tessa wasn't looking forward to. Mainly because she was now afraid that Gabe honestly wouldn't care. That he'd shrug and say, *Whatever you want.*

For all that was going right in her life, the Gabe things were coasting downhill from worse to worser. It wasn't as if he yelled or got mad or they argued or he wasn't nice. It was as if he wasn't there at all. And after having Gabe "be there" for four years, when he wasn't there anymore, Tessa felt as though she were living in some subterranean underworld where the skies were purple and the sun rose at night. It didn't feel right. And she tried to fix it. She coaxed, she smiled, she complimented and she seduced. Yeah, she seduced that man every which way but loose. But it didn't matter. Things were stubbornly stuck in reverse.

"I'll talk to him tomorrow."

Marisa lifted herself up in the chair and pointed a finger in what she thought was Tessa's general direction. "Don't let him talk you out of this."

Tessa smiled, cracking the cast on her face. "Don't worry. I don't think he'll even try."

TWO AFTERNOONS LATER, GABE was downstairs in the office, doing paperwork, when Tessa dropped by to see how the expansion was going. He wasn't sure why she'd come, but he knew by the way she was standing that something was up.

She made small talk. Asked about the permit, when things were going to open, yada yada and all he wanted to ask was *Why are you here?*

Eventually she got around to the thing that was putting the danger in her stance.

"I've got a chance to buy my place at Hudson Towers."

The pencil in his hand snapped in two pieces. Gabe took a deep breath—which was difficult when a man gets kicked in the nuts once again.

"What do I have to do with this?" he asked, because if she asked his advice or asked what he thought about it or asked if he had any objections, it wouldn't hurt so bad. It would still hurt, mind you, but it wouldn't kill him.

"I wanted to tell you in person. It's the smart thing to do. It'll be a great investment, way to plan for my future."

Smart. Future. Tessa. They were such foreign concepts to the old Tessa. The one that he loved. As much as he loved the new one, too, he wasn't sure his heart could take the wear and tear.

"You know, before we started up together, I was fairly confident, and lots of women liked me like that. But you make it very hard to retain even the smallest bit of pride, and that wears a man down over time."

Tessa stared as though he'd grown an extra head or something. "That's not true."

The fact that she actually believed it wasn't true made him

even madder. Good God, what did it take for her to open up her eyes? Did she think he would sit in this holding pattern forever? "Are you sure it's not true, Tessa? Are you really sure? Let's trace back, shall we? That first night, you wanted to sleep with anyone but me. *Anyone, including Stevie Tagglioli, the dark lord of cheesiness.* If it hadn't been so damned good between us, I would have walked away then. But after that one night I kept thinking, she'll figure this out on her own, give her some time. You've had it rough in the past, and I knew what I was stepping into. But then it gets worse. You had to pretend I was someone else every time we made love."

Gabe snapped the pencil again, just so she could get the visual reminder. "I got over that one, too, because I knew there was something about me that put the fear of God in you and I wasn't sure what it was, but I was willing to keep going. And if that had been the last hurdle, I think I'd still be okay—but, no, the list keeps getting longer. The next little stick in my eye? You throwing me at Marisa in exchange for an apartment. That one still stings, Tessa. But I know how much you wanted that place, and I'll be damned if I'm going to be jealous of a piece of real estate. So now we're here. Sleeping together once a week and not much else. You've got your future all mapped out, but where do I fit in, Tessa? Do you want me in your life or not?"

"You know I do." She crossed her arms across her chest, looking guilty, but he could see the gears rolling in her brain. And it dawned on him that Tessa really didn't know exactly where he fit in. He was the one destination on her life map that she had never considered.

He should leave now. Give her more time to work things out. But he couldn't do this anymore. He couldn't keep quiet now that all the words had started to flow. "How, Tessa? Where do we go from here? Do I have to pack a change of clothes once a week for the rest of my life? Is that what you're thinking? Because that's not good enough for me."

She pulled at a piece of her hair, looking so unsure and so much the way she'd looked four years ago when she'd walked into his bar. "What do you want?" she asked.

You. It was so simple to him, but her face was pale, her eyes were too big, and he wondered if it would ever be that simple for her. Probably not, but he was going to try one last time. Gabe took a deep breath and bet everything that he had.

"I want you with me, Tessa. Every day. Every night. I want to wake up with you in the morning, and watch you come to life after your second cup of coffee. I want to have to shuffle through the mess of your clothes on my desk. I want to meet you for lunch sometimes and hear about the boring details of your day. I want to know that you'll be next to me after I come home from closing up. Before you moved in with me, I was comfortable with my life, but not anymore. I don't want to live alone anymore. I hate it because you're not there. You know what's really pathetic? My pillow still smells like your shampoo, and every night before I get into bed I worry that today's the day it won't smell like you anymore. I don't want that day to come. Ever."

It was the longest speech he'd ever made in his entire life, and he took a deep breath, scanning her face for something. Some flash of recognition, some emotion, some bit of anything that would give him hope.

"Wow," she said in the same robotic tone that he knew and hated with a passion.

Damn.

"Ah, yes, wow. I can see this was a mistake. I'll leave now," Gabe said, burying his last bit of pride six feet under.

He opened the door and Tessa spoke. "I'm scared."

Gabe turned, looked at her. "Do you love me?"

"Yes."

He watched her, willing her to say something else, any
thing else, a baby step toward him, but she didn't. She only
stood there, stuck in Tessa purgatory, where it wasn't heaven
and it wasn't hell. Gabe swore. "How's time going to change
that, Tess?"

"It won't change my feelings, but it will change me."

"How? What are we waiting on here?"

"I don't know."

"Then how will you know you've changed?"

"Because I won't be scared."

"Why shouldn't you be scared? I'm terrified. I keep think
ing that you're going to wake up one day and not worry about
calling me or seeing me and it won't matter to you. And then
another day will go by, and eventually I'll be one of the old
lovers that you see on the street and you don't remember my
last name. That's what love is, Tessa, it scares the hell out of
you. And if it doesn't, I don't think it's love."

"I'm not ready," she whispered, and he could see the ice
in her eyes. That cold fear. Four years had passed since Denny
and she was still terrified. Gabe wouldn't wait around another
four years, not if it meant he had to live in this fucking limbo.
This was it. He'd called his own bluff and lost.

"'Bye, Tessa," he said. And this time he meant it.

14

A FEW DAYS LATER Tessa went to Prime to pick up her last paycheck. She didn't need it, but it was a handy excuse to see Gabe. Unfortunately, while her check was waiting for her in a neatly addressed white business envelope, Gabe was not. However, Jennifer and Cain were tending bar, Jennifer trying to relate to Cain about how real women drank mango margaritas, not cosmopolitans anymore.

As usual, there were the afternoon irregulars—Charlie, Lloyd, EC and Syd. Tessa took a moment to breathe in the familiar air, soak up the familiar sights. It was like coming home. Tessa pulled up a stool at the bar and bought a round for the men.

"You should come in every day," EC told her. "Think of how much money we'd save. We could give to charitable causes—"

"I'm a charitable cause," interrupted Syd. "You should give more to me."

"You're a civil servant. You don't need no charity."

"You're all civil servants," corrected Tessa.

"And we all need charity," answered Syd. "So the next round is on Tessa, too."

Tessa smiled, happy to be back home. Three hours passed, and there was still no sign of Gabe, but in walked someone else.

Kristine Langford and her great-aunt, Irene.

Tessa noticed first because she was a bartender and, as such, always spotted a new customer immediately. But it didn't take long for Syd to poke Charlie in the back. And just like before, the men sat there, whispering, and did absolutely nothing.

What would they do without Tessa?

She asked Cain to make an appletini for Kristine and, she suspected, a Sinagapore Sling for her great-aunt. Irene Langford carried herself in that way an older woman did when she'd been a great beauty in her day. There was confidence, pride and complete belief that the world considered itself lucky that she were part of it. Tessa stared in awe.

When she was eighty-something, she wanted to carry herself like that, too.

She took the drinks and walked carefully, royally, over to the Langfords' table. "I've brought you drinks. Kristine says that you're Irene Langford—is that correct?"

The old woman arched an eyebrow. "Do we know you?"

"I've met your niece, but I know a gentleman who's been looking you for you for what I suspect is a long, long time."

Kristine leaned over to her great-aunt. "She's the bartender I was telling you about."

Irene Langford gave Tessa a careful once-over, and Tessa only hoped she passed. "Who is this gentleman?"

"Charlie Atwood."

"I told you already, Aunt Irene," started the younger woman, and her aunt interrupted her with a look.

"In my day, you did not assume too eager or too knowing." Then she turned back to Tessa. "Who is this gentleman?"

"Charlie Atwood," repeated Tessa, gesturing for Charlie to come over. It took more whispering and poking and male primping, but Charlie ambled over, carefully, yet futilely tucking in his bulk.

He made it to the table and nodded politely.

"Do I know you?" Irene asked him.

"I think so, but I don't know from where."

"I've been a lot of places, mister, and covered a lot of years, so it could be anywhere, and you don't look familiar to me."

Charlie skimmed a hand over his head. "I had hair once, a full head of dark hair. And was about fifty pounds lighter. And no glasses."

"Take off your glasses."

He obeyed, and Irene stared before shaking her head. "It still doesn't help me."

But Charlie wasn't about to quit. "Have you been here before?"

"A long time ago. When it wasn't this den of iniquity. It used to be classy."

"Irene, I knew it was here. Before the war. You *have* to remember, Irene." The second time that he said her name he sat down next to her, caught her hand. At first she pulled it away, but Charlie held tight. He wasn't letting go.

"Yes?"

"Do you remember a song, 'All or Nothing at All'? It was playing on the radio."

She frowned, drawing gray brows together in a line. "On New Year's Eve? I was dancing that night, in the most glorious blue dress."

"White," he corrected.

"It was blue."

"It was white, and you smelled like lilacs."

Her head tilted and her lips curved into a young girl's smile. "I did love my lilac perfume."

Charlie clasped her hand tighter, his normally lighthearted voice colored with an emotion that Tessa had never heard before. "I kissed you at midnight."

"A proper lady doesn't kiss a stranger," she answered back with a hint of rebuke.

"I told you that within a month we'd be married and you

wouldn't have to worry about that anymore. I was supposed to meet you at the park the next day."

Suddenly recognition dawned in her faded blue eyes. "Charles? *Charles?* That was you, wasn't it? After all these years…I waited for you. For three weeks I waited for you to come calling, but you were never there."

"Uncle Sam shanghaied me to the Pacific. I didn't have a choice."

She put a shaking hand to her mouth. "You were a handsome gent, all in your whites and so thin."

Charlie lifted her hand to his lips, and the bar was so quiet you could hear a pin drop…or a heart sigh. The two gray heads huddled together, and they began to talk as if sixty years had never happened.

Tessa leaned her chin on her palm, her eyes misty, too. That was true love. Sixty years in the making.

Sixty long years of waiting. Sixty long years of waiting to be with someone that you loved.

Then Tessa started to smile, she started to grin, she wanted to sing. It would be a stupid, stupid woman to wait sixty long years to be with someone, and Tessa Hart—the new, improved Tessa Hart—was not stupid at all.

GABE HATED FEELING GUILTY. Mostly he hated feeling guilty when he didn't think he *should* feel guilty. Why did he feel like the bad guy? He was tired of hurting, he was tired of taking second place, he was tired of being alone and he was tired of keeping everything loaded up inside of him.

He wanted his heart back, but he wasn't sure it would ever fully be his again. Sean would laugh, Daniel would preach and Uncle Pat would raise his glass. Every man dealt with love in a different way, but Gabe wasn't used to falling in love like his brothers, and if this was how love is, well, it stank.

However, Gabe wasn't a dope, either. The hard facts were

that he loved Tessa. The old Tessa. The new Tessa. The fat Tessa. The skinny Tessa. The mommy Tessa. The career-track Tessa. The cat-owner Tessa. The electrician Tessa. The bartender Tessa. The real-estate-tycoon Tessa.

He loved them all because it really didn't matter what she wore or what she didn't wear or what name was tattooed on her butt or what animal she kept in her house or where she lived. He loved her and, yes, he was tired of being second choice, but he knew that someday he would be her first choice. Because Tessa, as much as she didn't believe it, was as constant as a 4:00 a.m. last call. You might be dead on your feet when it came around, but you knew it was going to happen, like sunrise, like sunset, like Tessa.

She loved him. That was the important message to remember. So she wanted him to wait? Suck it up, O'Sullivan. He was going to wait and hope to hell that he didn't have a heart attack at twenty-nine. He was going to wait forever if he had to, and his impatient streak would have to learn some pateince.

With all that decided, Gabe went over to her apartment at Hudson Towers. His noble speech was all planned out in his head, and he didn't even grit his teeth or feel the anger vein pop out on his forehead at the sight of her building. She liked this place for a reason, and it was probably a smart reason because nobody knew apartments like his Tessa. That made him smile, but his smile dwindled to nothing because she wasn't there when the doorman buzzed him in. Probably out showing an apartment to some Wall Street hedge-fund manager who needed a mistress, and he would hit on her and…

Stop.

Tessa could take care of herself.

Instead he went upstairs and left a note duct-taped to her door. *I love you. Gabe.*

It wasn't much, but she'd figure it out. This new Tessa? She was smart. That momentous, life-changing decision taken care of, he walked the thirty-three short blocks and seven long blocks from her place to his. Tessa wanted to buy into real estate? He'd deal. She wanted to open a candy store? He'd deal. She wanted to fly to the moon? He'd deal. Actually, for that one, he'd probably want to go, too.

As he walked, Gabe practiced his understanding face, practiced biting his tongue, practiced asking about her day…because, dammit, he tended bar, and in the entire planet there was no man more understanding than a man who tended bar.

WHEN HE GOT BACK TO his building, Tessa was camped out on his doorstep, sitting on three boxes, a suitcase and one mattress that looked as if it'd been dragged on the subway. Gabe didn't want to leap to conclusions, but in his heart conclusions were jumping up and down, east and west and all points in between

"You're here," he said carefully.

"I came home," she answered equally as carefully.

"Did you get lost?"

"Nope. Got found."

"Wow," he said, because this made him nervous. There was a catch in here somewhere, he just didn't know what it was.

"You going to let me in or do I have to sit out here like a homeless person? Which I am now officially, by the way, but I'd rather not let people know it." She pointed to the cat that was currently climbing out of her backpack. "Does your building take pets?"

"I don't know," he answered, stupidly trying to remember the building's rules and regs, all the while processing the fact that this time there seemed to be no catch. "You're here."

"Yep, Sherlock. I'm here. To stay."

"Why?" he asked, still waiting for the catch.

"You haven't figured out the *why* yet Gabe?" she asked, and he scanned her face, locked on her eyes, read the signs reflected in the perfect green depths…and—holy shit—there was no catch.

Slowly he began to smile. "I think I have, but I need you to tell me. Actually, my tenderized ego needs you to tell me, I don't actually need you to, but I want to hear it anyway."

"I don't want to wait. I'm done. From here on out, everything in my life is gravy, and I don't need to wait on the gravy. I want to go to sleep next to you, I want to wake up next to you, I want to share your shower and eat your food. I want to know that I can go into Prime and you'll take me into the office and have your wicked way with me anytime I want."

"Anytime?"

She nodded. "Anytime."

"I like that," he said, keeping his features perfectly schooled.

"I thought you would since all this was your idea after all."

"You remember that?"

"You were right."

"Music to my ears."

"I love you, Gabe. I've loved you for four years because you're the only man in New York who believed that I was a strong and capable person—and you were right."

"You just remember that I'm always right," he told her, then remembered his earlier resolutions and corrected himself. "Not always."

"Are you going to kiss me?"

Gabe shook his head. "Once I start, I don't think I'm going to stop, so I need to get all the talking out of the way first."

"You have a lot of talking to do?"

"A little. I was going to wait for you. I was going to tell you to take the place if it'd make you happy—and there's a note on your door to prove it, in case you don't believe me."

"I believe you. You look too proud to be fudging the truth."

"Do you want to buy the apartment at Hudson Towers?"

"No."

"No, that's not what I meant. Let me clarify. Would you rather live there than here?"

"You'd sell your place?"

For her, he'd sell his bar, his left nut and possibly his brothers. His apartment was an easy choice. "I don't know. You know your stuff. You tell me what's the right thing to do."

"You're kidding? You're sitting on half a million dollars worth of real estate and you're entrusting it to me?"

"Yes."

"Oh, my God. You love me."

"You finally figured that out?"

She brushed back tears. Only Tessa would cry about an apartment. It only made him love her more. "I think we should sell out this place and buy a two-bedroom in Hudson Towers."

Instantly the warning alarm sounded. "Two bedrooms? No way. No frigging way."

Tessa held up a hand. "Hear me out. There'd be our room. And Caesar's room, which would also be an office. And you can get a hugely bigger return on a two-bedroom than a one-bedroom. Although a three-bedroom? That's like the golden unicorn of the New York apartment, and if we could swing a three-bedroom…"

"You decide," he said, thinking that property taxes on a three-bedroom would be killer, and that that many rooms would be a bitch to keep clean.

"Let's do a two bedroom."

"Whatever you say, dear."

"I like the sound of that."

"Before you start pulling out your contracts, come here."

"My stuff is still out in the hall."

"Your stuff can wait. I've been waiting four years."

Wisely making the Gabe choice, she came into his arms

as if she belonged there. And she did. He caught her chin in his hand and kissed her. Long, slow, deep and thorough, as though he had all the time in the world. Because now, with Tessa, he did.

* * * * *

Don't miss Daniel's story,
SEX, STRAIGHT UP
Coming next month!

Enjoy a sneak preview of
MATCHMAKING WITH A MISSION
by B.J. Daniels,
part of the **WHITEHORSE, MONTANA** *miniseries.*
Available from Harlequin Intrigue
in April 2008.

Nate Dempsey has returned to Whitehorse to uncover the truth about his past...

Nate sensed someone watching the house and looked out in surprise to see a woman astride a paint horse just on the other side of the fence. He quickly stepped back from the filthy second-floor window, although he doubted she could have seen him. Only a little of the June sun pierced the dirty glass to glow on the dust-coated floor at his feet as he waited a few heartbeats before he looked out again.

The place was so isolated he hadn't expected to see another soul. Like the front yard, the dirt road was waist-high with weeds. When he'd broken the lock on the back door, he'd had to kick aside a pile of rotten leaves that had blown in from last fall.

As he sneaked a look, he saw that she was still there, staring at the house in a way that unnerved him. He shielded his eyes from the glare of the sun off the dirty window and studied her, taking in her head of long blond hair that feathered out in the breeze from under her Western straw hat.

She wore a tan canvas jacket, jeans and boots. But it was the way she sat astride the brown-and-white horse that nudged the memory.

He felt a chill as he realized he'd seen her before. In that very spot. She'd been just a kid then. A kid on a pretty paint horse. Not this one—the markings were different. Anyway, it couldn't have been the same horse, considering the last time he had seen her was more than twenty years ago. That horse would be dead by now.

His mind argued it probably wasn't even the same girl. But he knew better. It was the way she sat the horse, so at home in a saddle and secure in her world on the other side of that fence.

To the boy he'd been, she and her horse had represented freedom, a freedom he'd known he would never have—even after he escaped this house.

Nate saw her shift in the saddle, and for a moment he feared she planned to dismount and come toward the house. With Ellis Harper in his grave, there would be little to keep her away.

To his relief, she reined her horse around and rode back the way she'd come.

As he watched her ride away, he thought about the way she'd stared at the house—today and years ago. While the smartest thing she could do was to stay clear of this house, he had a feeling she'd be back.

Finding out her name should prove easy, since he figured she must live close by. As for her interest in Harper House… He would just have to make sure it didn't become a problem.

* * * * *

Be sure to look for
MATCHMAKING WITH A MISSION
and other suspenseful Harlequin Intrigue stories,
available in April
wherever books are sold.

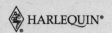

INTRIGUE

WHITEHORSE MONTANA

No matter how much Nate Dempsey's past haunted
him, McKenna Bailey couldn't keep him off her mind.
He'd returned to town to bury his troubled youth—
but she wouldn't stop pursuing him until he was
working on the ranch by her side.

Look for

MATCHMAKING
WITH A
MISSION

BY

B.J. DANIELS

*Available in April
wherever books are sold.*

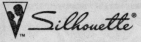

Silhouette®

Romantic
SUSPENSE

*Sparked by Danger,
Fueled by Passion.*

The Taken

Tierney Doyle is used to being criticized for
her psychic abilities, yet the tough-as-nails—
and drop-dead-gorgeous—detective has no doubt
about what she has uncovered in the case of a
string of unsolved murders. And Tierney is slowly
discovering that working so close to her partner,
detective Wade Callahan, could be lethal.

Look for

Danger Signals
by Kathleen Creighton

Available in April wherever books are sold.

nocturne™

The Bloodrunners
trilogy continues with book #2.

The hunt meant more to Jeremy Burns than dominance—
it meant facing the woman he left behind. Once
Jillian Murphy had belonged to Jeremy, but now she was
the Spirit Walker to the Silvercrest wolves. It would take
more than the rights of nature for Jeremy to renew his
claim on her—and she would not go easily once he had.

LAST WOLF
HUNTING

by RHYANNON BYRD

Available in April wherever books are sold.

Be sure to watch out for the last book,
Last Wolf Watching, available in May.

SN61785

REQUEST YOUR FREE BOOKS!

2 FREE NOVELS PLUS 2 FREE GIFTS!

HARLEQUIN®

Blaze™

Red-hot reads!

YES! Please send me 2 FREE Harlequin® Blaze™ novels and my 2 FREE gifts (gifts are worth about $10). After receiving them, if I don't wish to receive any more books, I can return the shipping statement marked "cancel". If I don't cancel, I will receive 6 brand-new novels every month and be billed just $4.24 per book in the U.S. or $4.71 per book in Canada, plus 25¢ shipping and handling per book and applicable taxes, if any*. That's a savings of 15% or more off the cover price! I understand that accepting the 2 free books and gifts places me under no obligation to buy anything. I can always return a shipment and cancel at any time. Even if I never buy another book, the two free books and gifts are mine to keep forever.

151 HDN ERVA 351 HDN ERUX

Name	(PLEASE PRINT)	
Address		Apt. #
City	State/Prov.	Zip/Postal Code

Signature (if under 18, a parent or guardian must sign)

Mail to the **Harlequin Reader Service:**
IN U.S.A.: P.O. Box 1867, Buffalo, NY 14240-1867
IN CANADA: P.O. Box 609, Fort Erie, Ontario L2A 5X3

Not valid to current subscribers of Harlequin Blaze books.

Want to try two free books from another line?
Call 1-800-873-8635 or visit www.morefreebooks.com.

* Terms and prices subject to change without notice. N.Y. residents add applicable sales tax. Canadian residents will be charged applicable provincial taxes and GST. This offer is limited to one order per household. All orders subject to approval. Credit or debit balances in a customer's account(s) may be offset by any other outstanding balance owed by or to the customer. Please allow 4 to 6 weeks for delivery. Offer available while quantities last.

Your Privacy: Harlequin Books is committed to protecting your privacy. Our Privacy Policy is available online at www.eHarlequin.com or upon request from the Reader Service. From time to time we make our lists of customers available to reputable third parties who may have a product or service of interest to you. If you would prefer we not share your name and address, please check here. ☐

HB08

COMING NEXT MONTH

#387 ONE FOR THE ROAD Crystal Green
Forbidden Fantasies

A cross-country trek. A reckless sexual encounter. Months ago, Lucy Christie wouldn't have considered either one a possibility. But now she is on the road, looking for thrills, adventure...sex. And the hot cowboy Lucy meets on the way seems just the man for the job....

#388 SEX, STRAIGHT UP Kathleen O'Reilly
Those Sexy O'Sullivans, Bk. 2

It's all on the line when Catherine Montefiore's family legacy is hit by a very public scandal. In private, she's hoping hot Irish hunk Daniel O'Sullivan can save the day. He's got all the necessary skills and, straight up or not, Catherine will have a long drink of Daniel any way she can get him....

#389 FRENCH KISSING Nancy Warren
Lust in Translation

New York fashionista Kimi Renton *knows* sexy photographer Holden McGregor is a walking fashion disaster. And she's tried to make him over. But when they're lip-locked it's *ooh la-la* all the way!

#390 DROP DEAD GORGEOUS Kimberly Raye
Love at First Bite, Bk. 2

Dillon Cash used to be the biggest geek in Skull Creek, Texas—until a vampire encounter changed him into a lean, mean sex machine. Now every woman in town wants a piece of the hunky cowboy. Every woman, that is, except his best friend, Meg Sweeney. But he'll convince her....

#391 NO STOPPING NOW Dawn Atkins

A gig as cameraperson on Doctor Nite's cable show is a coup for Jillian James and her documentary on bad-for-you bachelors. But behind the scenes, Brody Donegan is sexier than she expected. How can she get her footage if she can't keep out of his bed?

#392 PUTTING IT TO THE TEST Lori Borrill
Blush

Matt Jacobs is the man to beat—and Carly Abrams is determined to do what it takes to outsmart him on a matchmaking survey—even cheat. But Carly's problems don't *really* start until Matt—the star of her nighttime fantasies—wants to put her answers to the test!